Kathy

SPRINGSONG ❧ BOOKS

Andrea

Anne

Carrie

Colleen

Cynthia

Gillian

Jenny

Joanna

Kara

Kathy

Lisa

Melissa

Michelle

Paige

Sherri

Kathy

Marcia Mitchell

BETHANY HOUSE PUBLISHERS
MINNEAPOLIS, MINNESOTA 55438

Kathy
Marcia Mitchell

Library of Congress Catalog Card Number
applied for

ISBN 1–55661–610–4

Published by Bethany House Publishers
A Ministry of Bethany Fellowship, Inc.
11300 Hampshire Avenue South
Minneapolis, Minnesota 55438

Printed in the United States of America

To my daughter Kathie,

because I love you

MARCIA MITCHELL, born and raised in the Pacific Northwest, is a writer, speaker, and minister. She has authored several fiction and non-fiction books as well as numerous articles, in addition to speaking at retreats and conferences. She is married and has two grown daughters and two grandchildren. She and her husband, Fred, a retired fire captain and former mayor and city councilman, are avid collectors of antiques and western art and live in the state of Washington.

1

Flying!

There was nothing so exhilarating, so stimulating, as slicing through the air. Kathy Evans banked her Cessna toward the La Grande airport. Together she and the airplane dropped out of the sky to rejoin the earth. Coasting to a stop, she popped open the door and stepped onto the warm tarmac. Dodging clear of the now-still propeller, Kathy felt the wind ruffle her honey blond hair. It was good to be back in the Blue Mountains again. Those last four years at college had seemed endless. Now she slowly released her breath, letting the tension slip away with the Oregon wind.

She raised hazel eyes to the snow-topped mountains towering above her tiny frame and flicked a blond strand out of her eyes. A verse her dad often quoted rang in her mind: "I lift up my eyes to the hills—where does my help come from? My help comes from the Lord, the Maker of heaven and earth." She nodded her head gently at the memory. His favorite Bible verses had become a part of her, too.

Kathy brushed her hand across her forehead and shaded her eyes. Just beyond this rim of cobalt mountains lay the majestic Wallowas . . . and Jed. Anticipation stirred her emotions. In just moments she'd be seeing him again. "I wonder if he's changed," she mused.

Her emerald scarf brushed her long eyelashes as it flapped in the wind. She tucked the errant tip under her jacket and stuffed her hands into the pockets of her cream

7

pants. The morning air brought a fresh strawberry pink to her cheeks.

Sighing again, Kathy turned away from the mountains to seek out her passenger. She ducked under the wing of her single engine Cessna and reached inside the cab for her orders, confirming the name and destination. At least the summer promised to be fun. Charter flights for her father's business were usually more fun than work.

If there was one thing she loved, it was flying. From their home in Pendleton, Oregon, Kathy and her father often flew to smaller communities, ferrying passengers and packages to outlying destinations. Today, her first flight of the season had brought her to the nearby community of La Grande. It was a double-duty flight to pick up both a passenger and a package and deliver them over the mountains to the Joseph Airport. The package for Jed was just the excuse she needed to drop in and see him.

"You're the pilot?" A deep voice carved the air just inches behind her.

"Mr. Kingston?" She whirled to face her passenger and abruptly stepped backward to look up into his face. The sparks in her eyes fused instantly with the deepest blue eyes she'd ever seen. Suddenly she was drowning and didn't know why. Her breath caught somewhere near her midsection and refused to budge. Eventually survival forced her to draw a ragged breath.

"If . . . if you'd rather have a male pilot," she stammered, "I can get one for you. But it'll take about an hour for the extra round trip."

"That won't be necessary." His eyes refocused on her mouth, then slowly raised to lock with her gaze again. "I'm sure you can fly, or Mr. Evans wouldn't have sent you."

"It's worse than that," Kathy let a slow smile warm her face, "I'm Kathy Evans. My father taught me how to fly."

Reaching back through the open cab door to unlock the

passenger door, Kathy noticed her hands were shaking. Puzzled at the effect of such a short encounter with this stranger, she sought a few moments away from him to sort out her reaction.

"Go ahead and get in," she directed, "I have to pick up a package in the shop. But please don't touch anything while I'm gone."

"Anything I can help you with?" he asked, tilting his head to one side. His voice was deep and warm, his smile gentle. Kathy had the feeling he could have helped her pack the whole world in a box if she asked him. When she shook her head no, he turned away from her, skirted the Cessna's tail, and climbed into the right side.

Outdoors type stuffed in a business suit. Kathy silently played her usual guessing game, noting the open collar at his neck. *About thirty or so.* Broad-chested, lean, and muscular, with brown hair waving gently back from his wide tanned forehead.

Realizing that she'd been staring at him, she turned her back to him. But the few moments that it took to reach the hangar weren't enough to restore her usual calm or allow her to explain the strange reaction she'd just experienced. It was as though she'd been caught in a powerful magnetic force. Whatever it was, she decided, she'd just have to ignore it. They would only see each other for a few minutes. It wasn't as though she'd be spending the rest of her life with him.

Entering the darkened hangar, Kathy found the package on the mechanic's workbench where Jed had told her it would be. She hefted the box. It was small but heavy, clearly marked with a note that said, *For Jed James. Hope this is what you wanted. Jess.* She tucked it securely under her arm and retraced her steps to the waiting airplane.

There was a sudden gust of wind as she unlocked the baggage compartment in the tail section of the plane.

Brushing escaping strands of hair away from her eyes, Kathy automatically scanned the windsock to check its direction. She loaded Mr. Kingston's suitcase and added Jed's package, carefully locking the baggage compartment.

A quick walk around the plane assured her that the aircraft was still airworthy. When she climbed back into the cabin and started the preflight procedures, she ignored Mr. Kingston's open watchfulness.

"I just hope your father knows what he's doing." He tightened his seat belt. "I'm not in the habit of hiring teenagers to do a man's job."

"If it will help you relax, Mr. Kingston, I'm not a teenager." She sighed softly. "At the *advanced* age of twenty-two, I've completed college. And I've been flying charters for my father for the last three summers."

She avoided looking directly at his eyes. "I know this airplane inside and out . . . and these mountains"—she gestured toward the Blues and Wallowas beyond—"are as familiar as the sandbox in my parents' backyard."

Having satisfied herself that everything was ready, she slid her seat all the way forward and snapped on the seat belt. As usual she whispered a silent prayer for God's protection.

"Kind of tiny to handle this big machine, aren't you?"

"I assure you every bit of me is fully in control of this great big airplane!" Kathy glanced up from the panel and caught a twinkle in his eye. She slowly matched his grin.

"Seriously, Mr. Kingston," she offered in case his teasing was just a cover, "if you're the least bit uncomfortable, I can still get another pilot."

"I told you that wouldn't be necessary." He stretched his long legs into a more comfortable position. "As long as you can reach the rudders, that is."

"Have you flown much?" She was still struggling with

the magnetism that flickered between their eyes each time their glances met.

"Probably more than you have." He raised one eyebrow slightly, hesitated, then turned away from her. She had the distinct impression he'd started to say more, but changed his mind.

They rode in silence through the climb from the La Grande Airport. Leveling off, she changed the power setting, cutting down on the cabin noise.

In the eastern distance, just across the state border, Idaho's Seven Devil Range danced in the sun. Below them the mountain peaks were still covered with snow, even though it was late June. Oregon offered such a variety of landscapes. This section of mountains was a direct contrast to the open farmland just minutes away to the west.

Kathy briefly forgot her passenger as the eastern Oregon mountains slid silently beneath them. The morning sky gave a slick glaze to mounds of late snow, broken by tree-lined cleavages.

Deep at the bottom of a canyon off her left wing, the Minam Horse Ranch came into view. Tucked between shoulder-to-shoulder mountains, it was the only landing site in this rugged area.

"Ever land there?" Mr. Kingston's low voice broke the silence.

"Only once . . . when I was in training. It's a tricky approach. Not everyone should try it," Kathy explained, "but I always feel comfortable knowing it's within reach for a few minutes."

In reality, the loss of engine power in these mountains spelled sheer disaster, but Kathy didn't want to alarm him any more than necessary. Even with that grass strip below them, it would take a miracle to land unscathed in a real emergency.

"It's under new management," she continued talking

about the ranch. "But I haven't met the new owner." Her glance caught him staring out the window as the ranch drifted out of sight.

"Dad says this new owner flies a lot and plans to make the ranch available for church retreats. It's been a guest ranch in the past."

"If the man flies into that canyon," he commented dryly, "he's learned to pray." He shifted slightly, turning toward her and placing one long arm across the back of her seat.

For just an instant, Kathy felt his warm fingers brush the nape of her neck. Chills rippled down her spine. Shocked at the foreign sensation, Kathy swallowed to remoisten her dry mouth and tightened her stomach muscles to quell the butterflies. Then, as if suddenly realizing what he'd done, Mr. Kingston jerked his arm away and nervously clasped his hands in his lap.

For some unknown reason her emotions were a bit raw this morning. She was bouncing from a racing pulse to stomach jitters, and none of it was comfortable. *Maybe it's not him,* she mused. *Maybe I'm catching the flu.*

At last the checkerboard valley opened broadly beneath them, and Kathy banked toward the Joseph airport. She glanced briefly, longingly, at the saucer of blue cupped at the base of the Wallowa Mountains. The lake seemed to be welcoming her home. She hoped Jed would be watching and welcome her, too.

A warm sensation of joy prickled her skin as she tucked a neat landing pattern. Light as a butterfly, she touched down gracefully on the numbers and rolled to a stop at Joseph State Airport.

"Apparently you can fly," Mr. Kingston acknowledged her gentle landing.

"Any landing you can walk away from . . ." Kathy shrugged nonchalantly. She smiled graciously at him, then suddenly realized she was sorry the flight had ended so soon.

Kathy was pleased to arrive in plenty of time to see Jed. Not that it was really important, but this would be their first chance to see each other since the previous summer. She taxied to the end of the parking area near Big Mountain Aviation.

When she pulled his suitcase from the baggage compartment, Mr. Kingston slowly took it from her hands. Their fingers met briefly, and their eyes locked again. Pregnant silence reigned; he seemed about to say something important.

At last he whispered, "Thanks for a nice flight. See you around sometime."

She watched him toss his jacket and bag into a sleek sports car and leave without another word.

"Odd," she thought out loud, "I wonder what that was all about." She tied down the Cessna 172 and went in search of Jed. He wasn't hard to find. Jed stood on the aging wooden steps of the small office building, leaning against the cracked doorjamb. Short and wiry in his usual grease-streaked coveralls, he watched her approach, his red hair flaming in the morning light.

"You haven't changed a bit," she grinned as he pushed open a side door into the airplane shop.

"Did you bring the package?" Jed spoke tersely, stopping beside a torn-down engine.

"Sure. It's still out in the plane." Kathy frowned at his sharp tone. Somehow she'd expected a slightly warmer welcome.

"Thanks for bringing it to me on such short notice." His eyes darted toward the door, then bounced back to her.

"You know I'm always glad to deliver packages for you when they fit in with my flights. Just keep them smaller than an elephant!" Remembering the note attached to the package, she asked, "By the way, who is Jess?"

"A mechanic at La Grande." Jed's answer was now casual, and he wiped his arm across his forehead, trying to avoid the grease on his hands. "It's just some parts I need for a plane. He happened to have them on hand. And," he added in a more relaxed and completely normal tone, "to show you my gratitude, I'll treat you to a hamburger in town."

Kathy mentally shrugged in confusion over the unusual changes she saw in his tone and actions. She reached over and gave his curly red lock a gentle tug. "Thanks. I'll take you up on it!"

He started to reach for her hand, noticed the grease on his own, and shrugged apologetically. "I'm just a working man," he said, dropping his hand and reaching for a wrench. "I'm no match for Mr. Fancy and his racy sports car." He jerked a thumb to indicate Kathy's departed passenger.

"No need to apologize," Kathy countered. "Hamburgers are fine. In fact, why don't I go to town, pick them up, and bring them back here? That'll save you time, and I can still fly home this evening."

Kathy brought the package in from the airplane and gave it to Jed, then drove his battered pickup into town for the hamburgers.

On the way back to the airport, she was unable to shake the growing feeling that somehow Jed was different. She frowned slightly. *He seems to have changed, to be more . . . more withdrawn. No, that's not it either.* She dismissed the thought as she turned into the airport parking lot. "Maybe it's just that I've been away so long," she murmured.

2

$\mathcal{B}$y evening she was safely home in Pendleton and comfortably settled in the family room. An old schoolhouse clock, her mother's pride, ticked loudly in the quietness.

"You gonna marry him?" Peggy's high voice pierced the air.

"Who?" Kathy didn't even look up from the book she was reading. Her sister's questions were only a minor irritation.

"Who? Who? Who? That's what the owl said!" Peggy tossed a stuffed animal toward her.

Kathy caught it and tossed it back. "Sixteen is such an annoying age," she grimaced at her younger sister. "If you mean Jed . . . I don't know."

"Haven't seen you bring anyone else around. What's the matter, hasn't he asked you?" Peggy rolled over on the rug and sat up. She combed out her chestnut hair and coiled it on top of her head.

"That's none of your business."

"He hasn't, or you'd say so." Peggy twisted in front of the mirror over the couch. "Does this make me look older?"

"Quit wishing your life away," her father interrupted from the doorway. Playfully swatting Peggy with his newspaper, he smiled. "You're only sixteen once. Enjoy it."

Peggy made a face at them both and sashayed from the room. "That girl," he added, shaking his head. "I never know if she's going to be thirty-four or ten when I walk into a room!" He settled in the big flowered armchair and snapped open the evening newspaper. "Now you," he nodded at Kathy, "you were always sensible. Someone I could count on."

"Dad, sometimes I feel you think of me more as a *son* than a daughter." Kathy gave her dad a loving smile.

"Maybe so . . . but you'd make a good son, so what's the difference?"

They fell into a comfortable silence. Kathy glanced at her father, taking in his familiar brown cords and plaid sport shirt. She noted a few new lines across his forehead. Without his usual billed cap, his hair looked more gray than it had been at Christmas, although it still looked almost as blond as her own. Muffled sounds from the kitchen filtered into the room, followed by the pungent smell of warm chocolate.

"Mom's baking cookies." Kathy unfolded from the couch and abandoned her unread book.

"Don't eat them all," her father called from behind his paper.

"It's everyone for himself," Kathy teased. "I've been away from Mom's cooking too long." She reached the kitchen just as her mother pulled another pan from the oven. "Mmm . . . chocolate chip—my favorite!"

Her mother's warm brown eyes lit up softly as Kathy reached for a potholder to help. "It's nice to have you home."

"Nice to be home." Kathy took the pan and carefully removed the cookies onto a cooling rack.

"He hasn't asked her." Peggy's voice broke their shared moment.

"Peggy!" Her mother chided gently.

"Well, he hasn't. Just ask her yourself!"

"He who?" Their father joined the group at the table. "Hasn't *what*?"

"Peggy's making a big deal out of nothing—as usual." Kathy poured milk into four glasses and placed them on the round table. Adding a plate of cookies and a stack of napkins, she sat down in the chair next to her mother.

"I thought she'd come home from college and marry Jed." Peggy reached for a fresh cookie. "I even told Tanya I was going to be a bridesmaid. But now *she* says he hasn't even *asked* her yet."

"Well?" Her father raised a slow eyebrow in question, cookie paused halfway to his mouth.

"He hasn't asked," Kathy confirmed, washing down her cookie with a sip of milk. "We really don't know each other that well."

Still holding the cookie midair, her father looked squarely into her eyes. "Do you know where he stands spiritually?"

Kathy knew whenever her father had that look in his eyes that his question demanded a serious answer.

Peggy studied her long fingernails. "Jed always goes to church with you every time he comes to see you."

"Anyone can go to church," their mother interposed. "But that's no measure of a person's true spiritual condition." She shook a strand of chestnut hair back from her face.

Kathy noted the new threads of gray that made her mother's hair a little different from Peggy's. Mother and younger daughter looked alike, while Kathy strongly favored her father. Although they were divided in coloring, they had always been united as a family. If one of them had a problem, they all became involved.

"I don't have anything concrete to measure with." Kathy tapped the table with her fingertips and chose her words carefully. "Just a feeling that everything isn't exactly right. . . ."

"Enough to make you go slow." Her father patted her

hand with his large one. "Picking a husband or wife is a cautious business." He let go of her hand. "Besides, there's no rush. I can always use a good pilot."

"Why don't you hire that gorgeous guy from the Minam Horse Ranch?" Peggy stuffed another cookie in her mouth. "At least he's cute!"

"When do I get to meet this fantastic person?" Kathy relaxed at the slight change of subject.

"Mom wants you to meet him." Peggy licked the crumbs from her fingers. "She even showed him your high-school picture."

"Peggy!" her mother reprimanded and stood up to remove the empty dishes. "That's enough!"

"Well, you did," Peggy started to protest, then backed off at a stern look from her mother.

"I know you mean well, Mom." Kathy stood up too. "But I can find my own men. I can't stand being set up—it never works out." Whirling toward her sister, she added, "Whatever possessed you to tell Tanya you were going to be a bridesmaid? And, what is all this wedding talk, anyway? I've never even hinted at a wedding!"

"She's been hearing wedding bells all week," her mother answered. "Ever since we got the news that your cousin Kurt is engaged, Peggy can't talk about anything but weddings."

"Kurt's getting married?" Kathy exaggerated a shocked look. "I can't believe it. He's never mentioned anyone special. Who finally snagged him?"

"We haven't met her yet," her father spoke up. "She's from Seattle and was a student of Kurt's."

"Uh-oh," Kathy shook her head. "The old 'handsome flight instructor and student pilot' routine. I should have guessed."

"Her name's Jenny." Peggy threw her arms around

Kathy in a melodramatic hug. "And the way they met was so-o-o romantic."

"Everything's romantic to you." Kathy shrugged out of her sister's clasp. "Poor Jenny. Wait till she finds out Kurt is just an ordinary guy! I have a hard time thinking of Kurt as romantic."

"Just 'cause he's our cousin doesn't mean he isn't romantic." Peggy flounced back into her chair. "Anyway, we're going to go to their wedding. I can't wait to meet her."

Kathy grabbed an extra cookie and finished clearing the table. Thankful that the subject had shifted away from her and on to Kurt, she drifted out of the conversation and turned on the hot water in the sink.

———————

Late Wednesday morning, the telephone interrupted Kathy's daydreams and snapped her back to reality.

"Kathy?" A female voice sounded tentative, then confident. "I heard you were back in town, but I didn't believe it until now!"

"Lacey!" Kathy warmed instantly to her high-school chum's voice. "It's been ages. I've been meaning to call—"

"But you've been so busy!" Lacey finished the trite excuse. "Just because you've finally graduated from college doesn't mean you can ignore the most important person in your life!"

"You know I'm not ignoring you," Kathy accepted her friend's gentle chiding.

"Just teasing," Lacey explained, "but I'd love to see you. Any chance you can meet me for lunch?"

"Things are so quiet here I think Dad's snoring in his office." Kathy perked up at the invitation. "How soon can you break away from your shop?"

"Make it about half an hour. Mom can handle the customers while we're gone."

"It's almost as if nothing's changed," Kathy recalled their high-school days. "Whenever I think of your mother, I remember all the lovely dresses she'd let me try on. She spoiled me rotten every time I came into the shop."

"She always saved special dresses for you," Lacey agreed. "When we were unpacking a new shipment she'd say, 'Set aside that green one for Kathy.' Even now she starts talking about the old days whenever she sees a dress that would look good on you."

"Maybe I'll do a little shopping when we're through with lunch," Kathy glanced down at her well-worn jeans. "I'd love to see your mother again."

"I'd better not tell her," Lacey laughed, "or she'll have the whole back room stacked with clothes, each outfit selected just for you."

"I have to admit she runs the best dress boutique in town."

"Oops—gotta go," Lacey broke in. "Another customer just came in, and Mom's busy. Meet me at the Tea Room in half an hour."

Kathy tidied up her desk and poked her head around her father's door. His eyes were closed, but he wasn't sleeping. Noting his weathered hands folded on top of an open Bible, Kathy hesitated to interrupt his meditation. But some soft sound she made caused his eyes to fly open.

"Caught me praying," he smiled. "Did you need something?"

"Sorry to interrupt." Kathy leaned against the doorframe. "Lacey called and wanted to have lunch."

"Haven't seen her in a long time." He leaned back in his chair.

"If you can handle the load"—Kathy wryly indicated her empty office with a slight lift of one shoulder—"I'll go make amends with Lacey for not having called her sooner."

"Have fun." Her dad waved her out of the office. "I'll

try to struggle along while you're gone."

Kathy followed the winding road to the base of the hill, then threaded her way through town. The aged buildings and narrow streets clogged with traffic were the warp and woof of downtown Pendleton. The familiar old buildings, some standing since prior to the turn of the century, welcomed her home.

She passed the sleepy railroad station and turned the corner to park in front of the Tea Room. Situated in one section of a renovated building, its ancient door and squeaky board floors gave an Old West atmosphere.

Kathy pushed open the heavy door with its stained-glass window and stepped inside. An aromatic blend of exotic teas, pungent herbs, and freshly baked pastries filled the air. The walls were covered with antiques, old photographs, and memorabilia from early Pendleton Roundup days.

Spotting Lacey at a tiny round table by the front window, Kathy wove through the lunch crowd to meet her.

"I couldn't wait to see you," Lacey grinned as Kathy approached.

"You haven't changed a bit." Kathy hugged her friend, noting the familiar pageboy cut of Lacey's brunette hair.

"How can you say that?" Lacey patted her slender hips in mock horror. "I've jogged and sweated off ten pounds of high-school fat!"

"Whatever you're doing, it looks good on you," Kathy slipped into the chair across from her. "And I love that blouse."

"It just came in a shipment last week," Lacey fingered the collar of her Persian blue blouse. "I couldn't resist! Clothes are still my downfall—as my bank account will prove!"

When they'd ordered steaming cups of spiced tea and almond-topped croissants, the friends sat quietly for a moment, studying each other.

"Tell me everything," Lacey ordered, her blue eyes searching Kathy's hazel ones. "I want to hear about college, your love life, the whole thing."

"Didn't you read any of my letters?" Kathy laughed. "To hear you talk, a person would think I hadn't written to you nearly every week for the past four years!"

"That's history," Lacey broke off a small bit of flakey pastry and buttered it lightly. "I mean *now*. I couldn't get away for graduation, and no matter how much I've pried, you've been strangely silent about the men in your life."

"Graduation was typical," Kathy started to explain, stirring her tea.

"Then skip graduation for now," Lacey interrupted with a mischievous sparkle in her eyes. "Get down to the good stuff—men!"

"In this case, silence is the truth," Kathy shrugged. "I dated a variety of guys, but there never was anyone special."

"I don't believe it," Lacey shook her head. "The way you look, combined with the way you cook—I'd have thought they'd be standing in line."

Kathy sank her teeth into the warm croissant and slowly savored the almond flavor. Hot butter trickled over her fingers. "What about you? Anyone special?"

"Nothing new," Lacey shrugged in exaggerated tragedy. "In fact, nothing at all."

They sipped their tea, each one adjusting quickly back into their familiar friendship, openly accepting the inevitable changes.

"How are things with Jed?" Lacey eyed Kathy carefully.

"Not much happening." Kathy twisted her cup absently. "He hasn't answered my letters for months. I saw him on Monday, but he seemed different. I'm not sure I can explain it."

"But you keep hoping?"

"I'm just not sure about anything," Kathy sighed.

"What are your great plans now that you've finally graduated?" Lacey eyed a second croissant, but decided against it.

"I really don't have any," Kathy shrugged. "Guess I'll fly for Dad until I see some handwriting in the sky. Right now I don't seem to have much direction in my life. If I went to a big city, I could easily get a job with my business degree. But I love the quiet life here."

"What about all those wonderful lectures you wrote to me about?" Lacey countered. "Sure sounded as though you were getting enough direction there. Didn't you pay any attention to those professors?"

"Of course I did." Kathy grinned sheepishly. "I was just joking about the handwriting in the sky. But seriously, I guess I should at least go back to see Jed."

"Before you do"—Lacey relaxed again—"drop in at the shop and get some new clothes. It'll do wonders for your ego, and it can't hurt to look spiffy when you go to see him."

"I had planned to stop in today, but I've been gone so long already." Kathy glanced at her watch. "Dad'll be starved. Maybe I'll drop by and drag Peggy in with me. All she ever wears is jeans. It couldn't hurt to expose her to your mother's influence!"

3

*T*hursday morning the phone rang, shattering Kathy's concentration on a fuel invoice. "Can you go with me out to the Woolen Mills?" Peggy pleaded in her best sixteen-year-old way. "Mom says I have to get started on my wool suit for fall, and she doesn't have time to help me pick out any material. You're so good at it, I really need you."

The idea was tempting. Next to cooking, Kathy loved to sew, and she hadn't been out to the Pendleton Woolen Mills in a couple years.

"Give me an hour to finish these invoices," she agreed. "I'm sure Dad won't mind if I'm gone for a little while. Meet me here about one o'clock. I should be ready then."

Peggy arrived on time, which both surprised and pleased Kathy. Sliding into the passenger side of the car, she enjoyed her sister's pride at having a driver's license at last. Threading their way along the base of the hill, Kathy and Peggy wove through the back streets of Pendleton to the unpretentious Pendleton Woolen Mills. The large red-brick building squatted at an angle along the railroad tracks.

They parked against the fence and hurried up the cement steps, both of them eager to see the new selection of fabrics. Inside, they allowed their eyes to adjust from the bright sunlight to the soft interior lighting of the small room.

In the back, down a narrow hallway, Kathy could see the entry to the rooms where the famous Pendleton wool blankets were being loomed. But her attention shifted instantly to the rows of rolled wool hanging along the walls.

Plaids of red, black, green, and blue covered the wall to her right. A few rolls of plain colors, mostly green and brown, were on a rack just ahead, while off to the left, in a back corner, there were a few woven linen fabrics.

Kathy glanced briefly at the stacks of finished blankets in the section near the door. They would be eagerly snapped up by visitors and tourists when the famous Pendleton Roundup took place in the fall.

But for now, she concentrated on Peggy's wool suit.

"As lovely as that red is"—Kathy examined the fabric Peggy was fingering—"I don't think it's your best color."

"But I love it," Peggy pleaded. "And I don't have a red suit."

"Trust me," Kathy smiled ruefully at her sister. "Let's see if we can find something that will light up your face."

Kathy ran a practiced eye over the selections of wool, fingering a few and noting the texture and quality. Some were heavy, obviously intended for coats or blankets, while others were lighter.

"Come here a minute," she called Peggy away from the red. "Let me see what this does for you." She unrolled about a yard of cream wool with a subtle beige fleck.

"Umm, good," she murmured, "but I'm not sure you're ready to take care of a white suit."

"You know me too well," Peggy laughed. "I like it, but you're right. The first thing I'd do is get some stain on it. What about one of those brown ones?"

They both turned to a roll of finely textured brown and russet plaid at the bottom of the last row. Kathy rubbed the soft fabric between her fingers.

"It's light enough for a suit, and you could line it with a russet lining." She unrolled enough to hold up next to Peggy's face. "Oh, this is perfect. You should see how it brings the color to your face and lights up your eyes."

Peggy pulled even more fabric off the roll and draped it around her shoulders lovingly. "It's so soft, I love it."

While Peggy was buying the yardage, Kathy found a lightweight pale green remnant that would make a marvelous skirt for fall. When they had finished, the sisters piled their packages in the back of the car.

"Want to stop at Lacey's dress shop?" Kathy thought it would be a good time to help Peggy's sense of style.

"I don't have time," Peggy shook her head. "By the time I drop you off at the airport, I'll barely make it to band practice. We're working on a routine for the Roundup."

"Another time, then." Kathy let it go. It was enough for now that Peggy had allowed her to help select her suit fabric.

"Once in a while it's nice to have a big sister," Peggy grinned. "I just wish I had your skill at the sewing machine."

"You'll learn," Kathy ruffled her sister's hair as they pulled up in front of their office. "I kind of like having a sister, too. Who else can I practice on that won't scream if I make a mistake?"

"See you later," Peggy waved as Kathy got out of the car. She ground the gears slightly as she pulled out of the parking lot.

———

Restless one morning a few days later, Kathy wandered outside their office and sat on the steps to watch the airplanes. One, obviously piloted by a student, made endless circles around the airport as the novice practiced take-offs and landings.

"Just like me," she mused softly, "I go around and around every day doing the same things, but never seem to get anywhere."

"We all feel that way sometimes." Kathy twisted around at the deep, yet lilting, voice. A smile lit her face when she saw the tall, dark-haired stranger.

"Excuse me." Kathy jumped up to meet him. "I didn't know anyone was near. Can I help you with something?"

"It sounds as if I should be the one helping you," he countered and paused, obviously waiting for Kathy to take him up on his offer. When she didn't, he continued, "My name is Dr. Strauss, Jon Strauss. I'm a music professor from a college in Idaho, and I'm on my way to Wallowa Lake. I'm on staff for a church camp this summer."

"Oh," Kathy stammered slightly at such a full dose of information. "Did you want to charter a flight?" He seemed young to be a professor.

"Yes, I flew this far commercially. Any chance I could get somebody to fly me the rest of the way?"

"No problem." Kathy led the way into her office. "If we hurry," she added, "you'll be there in time for lunch."

He followed her closely and closed the door behind them. "Anytime you'd like to talk about . . . the things you were thinking about when I walked up, I'm willing to listen."

"Oh, it's really nothing." Kathy flashed him a puzzled smile. "Sometimes I wonder just what I'm doing with my life—or even with the hours in each day. It's probably just a letdown from all those intense weeks at school. I just graduated from college, and if you teach at one, I'm sure you know what I mean." She spread her hands, palms up in an offhand shrug.

"We can't always see the entire scope of God's plan for our lives." He watched her face carefully. "Sometimes we just have to take it a day at a time. And, you could be right; there's usually a letdown in the summer, especially right after graduation. What was your major?"

"Business administration." Kathy smiled, too, responding to his unasked question about her attitude toward God. "And you're right. I don't know what God's plan is." She shrugged and turned to fill out the proper paper work.

She made a quick phone call to her mother to tell her

where she was going. Her mind then skipped ahead to their destination. *Maybe this time when I see Jed,* she thought, *he'll be more like he was last summer.* She remembered him as being gentle and full of fun. A time or two Kathy had even thought he might be getting serious about her. But when he didn't answer her letters, she finally quit writing. At Christmas break there hadn't been time or good enough weather to fly into Joseph to see him.

She ushered the professor out to the airplane and loaded his baggage. In minutes they were airborne, and Kathy left her questions far below.

After delivering Dr. Strauss first to the airport, and then, borrowing Jed's pickup, finally to the church campgrounds at the lake, Kathy decided to have lunch before she flew home. She pushed open the door to a small restaurant and stood in line.

"It seems I can't get away from you, Miss Evans," a deep voice spoke just behind her shoulder.

Kathy whirled around and nearly bumped her nose on Mr. Kingston's chest. "You!" She caught her breath and was suddenly drenched in the scent of his cologne. There was a thickness in the air around him, and Kathy made herself back away from him.

"I should have known it was you, Mr. Kingston." She smiled at him. "Everyone else around here calls me Kathy."

"Are you suggesting I call you Kathy?" The twinkle in his eyes drew her attention like a beacon. Dressed in blue jeans and a plaid shirt, he stood with both hands resting lightly on his slender hips.

"No . . . that is, I—oh, just call me whatever you like." Kathy was surprised at her confusion.

"Actually, *Kathy*," he emphasized her name, "I was just going to find a telephone to call you."

Kathy raised an eyebrow and said nothing. She was used

to being asked for dates, but wasn't sure that was what he intended to ask.

"I need to make several more flights while I'm here," he went on quickly, "and I want you available to fly whenever I need you."

"We'll be happy to accommodate your flights," Kathy fought to keep her voice under control, "but I can't just sit here waiting. There are other charters to fly, and my home base is in Pendleton."

"I know," he shrugged apologetically, "but I *do* need you available at a moment's notice. I'll call your father and make some arrangements." He turned on his heel and strode away.

Kathy shook her head as he closed the door. *That man is a strange one,* she thought. Placing her order, she sat down at a table to wait until her hamburger was ready. She dismissed Mr. Kingston and his requests with the thought that her father would certainly tell him how impossible it would be for her to sit at an out-of-the-way airport waiting for a phone call. She was just coming out of the door when she heard him call her name again. She stood still, her hands holding the bag with her lunch in it, waiting for him to catch up to her.

"Your father agreed to my terms." He ignored the shocked look on her face and continued, "He said for you to fly home immediately and pack a bag. I'll meet you back at the airport in about two hours."

"I beg your pardon." Kathy just stood there, staring at him.

"Didn't you hear me?" His blue eyes searched her face.

"Yes . . . of course I heard you. It's just that . . ." her voice trailed off in confusion.

"What?"

"Oh . . . nothing." She held up the sack. "I was just going to have something to eat." She didn't want to tell him she didn't believe him. After all, she knew her father could not spare the airplane or the pilot. He'd made it very clear that he needed her to help him this summer. The best thing she could do was fly home and check with her father personally. Obviously there was some mistake.

"I'm not asking you to go hungry," he cocked one eyebrow at the sack and grinned. Then he added, "I'll be at the airport at seven this evening to pick you up."

Confused, Kathy drove back to the airport and stuck her head into the shop. "Wish I could stay and visit," she apologized to Jed who was bent over an engine, "but something's come up and I have to go home."

As an afterthought she added, "Here, have a hamburger. I don't have time to eat it."

"Kathy, wait," Jed called out, waving a wrench in her direction. "When will you be back?"

"I'm not sure," she answered over her shoulder.

But precisely at seven Kathy was landing back at Joseph, still very confused. Her father's reason was simple. Mr. Kingston had paid for the airplane and her services as a pilot.

"You're the only one I can send," her father had overruled her protests. "Besides, we need the business, and he offered far more than what we usually charge. He's the kind of person who, when he wants something, wants it now. It's just easier to have you there, ready to fly whenever he wants, than to wait and wonder if anyone is available. Remember, call if you need anything."

As she tied down the plane, she noticed the door to the aviation shop was padlocked. That meant Jed had gone home for the night, he wouldn't even know she was back. At least, not until morning when he saw her plane there.

She looked up as a familiar figure was striding toward her. Preparing herself for the impact of their meeting, Kathy momentarily wondered why she reacted so strongly whenever she was within a few feet of this man.

It's like hitting an air pocket, she thought, watching him walk across the tarmac. *You can't see it, but suddenly the airplane lurches crazily, sending your heart into your throat.*

"Glad to see you're punctual," he interrupted her thoughts.

"Mr. Kingston," she started, "I still don't understand. . . ."

He picked up her suitcase and started toward the car. "Don't you think you should call me Trevor? I mean," he grinned, "there's no need to be quite so formal. We'll be spending a lot of time together."

Kathy took quick steps to keep up with him, yet kept her distance. "I'd be happy to . . . *Trevor,*" she couldn't help but grin, too. "I could hardly call you anything other than Mr. Kingston. You didn't bother to tell me your name till now."

He opened the car door for her. "Do you always treat your customers so formally?"

"Only when they think I'm still a teenager," she referred back to their first encounter. "Usually anyone who thinks I'm that young"—she let her grin widen and slide up to her eyes—"is so *old* he deserves a great deal of respect!"

"You get five points for that one," he laughed and started the engine. "I deserved every word." As he drove toward town, Kathy took a moment to covertly study the tall man next to her. He seemed younger now that he wore jeans and a plaid shirt. He was slender and nicely proportioned for a man who was taller than six feet. In spite of herself, Kathy had to admit that he certainly was handsome.

Not cute like Jed, Kathy thought, then caught herself, surprised that she was comparing the two men.

4

"*Y*ou mentioned you just graduated from college."

"Uh-huh," she nodded, still staring out the window. "I've only been home a couple weeks.

"With a degree in . . ." he prompted.

"Business administration." She threw him a curious glance.

"It's a lot of money to spend just to learn how to add and multiply! You going to do anything special with the degree?"

"I had other reasons, too." Kathy defended, then looked to see if he was teasing again. He was. "I don't have any immediate plans." She was going to have to pay closer attention so she'd know if he was serious or teasing.

"I suppose your father was trying to marry you off."

"I suppose," she shrugged, giving him a mock poor-little-me look before turning back to the gorgeous view of the lake. Two could play this game. "You, of course, managed to avoid that tragedy."

"Of course," he responded slowly.

They drove along the arid moraine that edged the north shore of Wallowa Lake. Kathy drank in the sparkling blue scene. Formed by the movement of an ancient glacier, the lake still housed icy water even on the hottest July day. On the remaining circular sweep of the compass, the lake was guarded by piercing mountains, blue in the evening light with white icing tipping their peaks.

"They certainly are majestic, aren't they?" Trevor followed her upswept gaze.

"Uh-huh," she nodded. "But only from down here, or skimming them like we did when I first brought you here. But if you fly really high up, they don't seem quite so formidable. I guess it depends on your perspective." She smoothed her tan cotton chinos and crossed her legs, unconsciously relaxing.

When they entered the park at the far end of the lake, Trevor turned left, away from the lodge and campgrounds. Tall pines welcomed them, and Kathy felt as though she were coming home, everything looked so familiar. They drove silently past a tiny shop patterned after a Swiss Chalet.

Vacationers strolled along both edges of the road as they returned from boating on the lake or a trip to the top of the mountains on the cable cars. A man on a horse paused long enough to let their car turn onto a dirt and gravel road toward the creek. The water was high as Trevor slowed to cross on the aging one-lane log bridge.

They drove past the church camp where Kathy had taken Dr. Strauss. She started to tell Trevor about him, then changed her mind. After his remark about her father trying to marry her off, he would obviously misunderstand about Dr. Strauss. *Not that the professor isn't good-looking,* Kathy thought.

In a few minutes, Trevor stopped the car in front of a large, rustic log cabin. Unlike many of the cabins nearby, the grass was neatly trimmed and perfectly edged along a flagstone patio on one side. Just off to the left, a camper was tucked between the patio and a stand of pine trees.

It was already cool in this shaded side of the mountain, and Kathy was glad she'd packed a variety of clothes. A sweatshirt was always welcome as soon as the sun dropped from sight. She sighed softly as she stepped from the car.

"If it will make this any easier," Trevor responded to her sigh, "try to think of this as a paid vacation. The work won't be difficult." He led the way up the wooden steps and opened the cabin door. "The cabin is yours and the trailer is mine. If you don't mind, we can share the kitchen."

Kathy said nothing, but a smile flickered across her face as she followed him. He really was trying to make her feel comfortable.

She stopped just inside the door and surveyed the room. "Nice," she murmured. The entryway was slate, and to her left an open copper and knotty pine kitchen gleamed beneath swinging country lamps.

In front of her stretched a large, sunken living room with huge windows along the back wall and a monstrous stone fireplace at the far end. Two leather couches were smothered in brightly colored pillows, carelessly tossed and spilling onto the floor.

"Make yourself at home." Trevor was watching her with some amusement. "I'll just put your suitcase in your bedroom. It's the first door down the hall," he indicated.

"Thank you." She managed to smile. If the bedrooms were furnished anything like these rooms, she could hardly wait to see them.

For a moment after he was gone, the room dimmed and seemed to shift slightly. Kathy reached out a hand to steady herself.

"What's the matter? Are you all right?" Trevor's voice was far away as he stepped back into the room and saw her swaying toward the railing that separated the hall from the sunken room.

"Oh . . . I'm, uh . . . fine." Kathy concentrated carefully as the room came back into focus. "I don't know what's wrong. Nothing, I guess."

"When did you eat last?" Trevor's glance scrutinized her slender figure. He reached out to steady her shoulders.

"I had a cup of coffee this morning," she admitted lamely, "but I was in such a hurry to fly over here that I didn't bother to fix breakfast." If only her knees would quit shaking, she'd feel more confident.

"Is that all?" He led her to the couch and gently eased her into the cushions. "What about the lunch I saw you buy?"

"Actually, I wasn't exactly in a mood to eat at the time," she explained, "and I left my hamburger for Jed." Sitting down had helped her shaking knees.

"Just sit there till I find something to feed you." He dashed into the kitchen and began banging cupboard doors.

Kathy, feeling a little better, followed him just in time to hear him mutter, "There's nothing in the whole house to eat!"

"A cup of coffee will do fine," she said, leaning on the counter.

"Coffee!" Frown lines creased his brow. "There's no nourishment there. What if I need to fly somewhere tonight? Just how much confidence can I have in a pilot that's near starvation?" He opened the refrigerator and pulled out a meat tray. "Steaks. Great, but they'll take too long."

Kathy spotted some cheese slices on another shelf. "Why don't you let me fix something? I can manage okay—unless you want to eat, too?" It was a question she'd added almost without thinking. A sheepish look crossed his face.

"I didn't have time to eat, either." He shrugged, "Think you can scare up enough for both of us?" His tone had definitely softened.

Kathy shooed him out of the kitchen and nibbled on crackers and cheese while she put the steaks on to broil. There was plenty of food in the cupboards and refrigerator, and she smiled at his inability to find anything to eat.

At least he's not as self-sufficient as he'd like people to believe, she thought. Then, remembering his comment about needing her only to fly, she frowned. For some reason she was unable to define, Kathy felt a twinge of disappointment at his statement. *Not that I want any other kind of relationship with him,* she chided herself and turned the steaks.

It wasn't long before she'd tossed a crisp green salad, put two potatoes into the microwave to bake, and made a pot of coffee. Fortunately, the kitchen was a far cry from rustic. She mentally thanked whoever had created it.

"Do you want to eat in here?" She paused at the counter with the platter of steaks.

"No, I'll help you carry the plates into the living room." Trevor jumped up the two steps into the kitchen. They piled their plates with food, and Kathy balanced their empty cups while Trevor brought the coffeepot.

"Mmm, nice." Kathy viewed the chairs pulled comfortably in front of the fireplace. "Even in June a fire feels good in the mountains." She placed their cups on a low table made of a round piece of glass placed on top of a wagon wheel.

Trevor poured their cups to the brim, and they sipped the steaming brew cautiously. Silence filled the room as each one ate.

"Feel better?"

"Definitely!" She put down her fork and reached for her cup.

"More?"

"Thanks." She held it up, and Trevor filled it and his own again. They sat quietly, drinking their fill as they stared into the flames.

At last she stretched lazily and stood up. "I'd better tackle these dishes."

"No you don't." Trevor stood up too, shaking his head. "You cooked. I'll clean up."

"In that case"—Kathy glanced at her watch—"if you don't mind, I'll turn in. It's been a long day."

"Go ahead," he nodded, stacking their dishes. "I'll lock up when I'm done. If you need me, I'll be just outside in the camper."

Touching a light switch just inside the bedroom door filled the room with soft light. She caught her breath. She'd been right about the room. It glowed with the illusion of nearly a century past. One wall was dominated by a massive antique bed swathed in a green and cream print comforter. A matching dressing table and mirror was graced with a hand-painted antique lamp, electrified but real.

A curved couch in cream damask snuggled beside the woodburning stove, and one wall was filled with books. The remaining wall was covered floor to ceiling with matching cream drapes with only a fleck of green.

A print of an old painting of two children, a boy and a girl, crossing a treacherous mountain stream while a guardian angel hovered protectively was the only decoration. There was no clutter in the room, just sheer simplicity and elegance.

Kathy slid open a section of paneling and discovered an enormous walk-in closet next to a small but neatly arranged bathroom, complete with a claw-footed tub and shower.

Later, when she was on the edge of sleep, one last thought surfaced. Trevor had been concerned about her health because he needed her as a pilot. And, although there had been plenty of opportunities, he'd kept their relationship very businesslike. *At least that part is clear,* Kathy thought, wondering as she drifted into sleep why it didn't make her as happy as it should.

————

A soft tapping sound dragged her from the depths of sleep. "Kathy," came a whisper. "Kathy? Can you be ready to leave in an hour?"

"What time is it?" Kathy called toward the closed door.

"It's 4:30. I want to leave here no later than 5:30."

"Do I get to know where we're going?" Kathy raised up on one elbow, forcing herself fully awake.

"Spokane." His footsteps retreated down the hall.

So much for sleeping late, Kathy thought wryly. *And he called this a vacation?*

Moments later Trevor knocked on the door again. "What do you want for breakfast?"

"Nothing at this hour," she sputtered, playfully throwing a slipper at the closed door. Stimulated into a wide-awake state, she was ready in a record fifteen minutes.

She had slipped into a pair of toast-colored denims with an eggshell blouse and pinned golden wings on the edge of her collar. At the last minute, she added a hint of soft coral lipstick and brushed her honey gold hair one more time. Tucking her small Bible into her flight case so she could have devotions later, Kathy grabbed a light jacket. When she stepped out into the hallway, the pungent aroma of frying bacon drew her straight to the kitchen.

Seeing two plates set out on the table, Kathy glanced toward Trevor, who stood at the stove. A towel draped loosely around his middle, protecting his brown trousers and yellow sport shirt.

Trevor looked up and caught her staring at him. "If you're going to fly"—he indicated the plates—"you have to eat." He lifted the strips of bacon from the pan and set them out to drain. "If you'll cook the eggs, I'll pour us some coffee." He peeled off the towel. "Eggs need a woman's touch as far as I'm concerned."

"Do we have time for all this?" Kathy moved to the stove and started the eggs. "I thought you wanted to leave at 5:30."

"There's time. I just didn't know how fast you could move in the morning," he grinned.

"Not fast enough to keep you from fixing a man's breakfast!" Kathy retorted. "Just look at all that fat!" She shook her head in mock despair. "From now on, the kitchen is *my* territory."

5

*A*t the airport they tracked across the wet grass to the plane. Trevor unexpectedly followed her lead, loosening the chains on the airplane and dropping them with a noisy clank. She called Flight Service from the phone booth outside the office, jotting their information on her flight plan.

As she walked away from the phone, Kathy noticed the lock on the maintenance shop was open, and she stopped to stare at it.

"What's wrong?" Trevor called, but when she didn't answer he came striding toward her. "I said—"

"Shh! I know what you said." Kathy stood quietly beside the open lock. "When I left here last night, that lock was closed and Jed was gone. Now it's open."

"Who is Jud?"

"*Jed,*" she corrected. "He's the mechanic here . . . and a friend of mine."

"Well, maybe he came back later." Trevor took her arm and pulled her away. "No need to make a federal case out of an open door."

"I suppose you're right, he could have come back." She let him lead her away. "But maybe I should call him to check."

"At this hour? Don't be ridiculous!" Trevor climbed into the passenger side of the airplane. "Let's get this thing into the air."

Kathy gave one last worried look at the open lock as she

40

taxied past the shop. Then, everything else forgotten, she concentrated on flying.

The sky was smooth as silk, allowing their airplane to slice the heavens without even a ripple. Summer mornings often were the best flying of the year. Cool, clean air gave a solid ride before the undulating heat waves boiled invisibly upward. Their flight was uneventful and very quiet, two people comfortable in their silence, enjoying the scenery.

Once she caught him glancing sharply at her flight panel. *Maybe he's quiet because he's still uncomfortable flying with a woman pilot,* she thought. They landed at Spokane and tied down at the FBO.

"Where can I drop you?" Trevor slid into the driver's seat of their rental car.

"Wherever fits into your plans." Kathy really hadn't known what to expect; he had been absolutely silent about his plans during their entire flight.

"Well, I have a meeting at the office, and then the investigation may take a little while."

"Investigation? Sounds serious." Kathy raised her eyebrow and turned in the seat to watch him. "What are you? FBI?"

"Nothing so glamorous." Trevor shook his head and started the car. "Insurance."

"You mean you investigate accidents?"

"Something like that." He turned toward downtown Spokane, leaving the airport quickly behind.

"That explains why you needed me at a moment's notice. I wish I had something important to do." Deciding to take advantage of his talkative mood she added, "But what are you doing so far away from everything? Joseph, Oregon, isn't exactly the center of the world!"

"Vacation. The cabin and the camper at the lake belong to . . . a friend." He signaled and switched lanes. "Now, what do you want to do while I'm working?"

"Some vacation," she tried to keep the conversation going, "being constantly on call isn't very relaxing." When he didn't respond and silence filled the car, Kathy finally asked, "Couldn't I just go with you? I mean, an investigation sounds sort of intriguing."

"Bloodthirsty, huh?" He raised an eyebrow in surprise, but his twinkling eyes and matching smile helped her relax. "Sorry to disappoint you, but this time it's just a paper chase. However, if I have any blood 'n guts accidents, I'll be sure to take you along."

Kathy knew it wouldn't do any good to tell him that she really hated "blood 'n guts," as he so aptly put it. "Just drop me anywhere downtown," she decided, since he'd made it very clear that he didn't want her with him. "I'll find something to do. What time and where shall I meet you for the return trip?" She tried unsuccessfully to keep the bored tone from her voice.

"Why don't I meet you at noon in the lobby of the Ridpath? We can have lunch, and I'll know more by then about our schedule."

"Okay." She nodded an acknowledgment as he pulled over to the curb.

By ten minutes before twelve Kathy was turning the corner a half block away from the Ridpath Hotel. She shifted her packages to the other arm, sternly chastising herself for buying so much. She had plunged into shopping after having a quiet cup of coffee and reading her Bible at a tiny hole-in-the-wall cafe. The wind blew her hair across her eyes, and when she brushed it away, she dropped the box containing her new dress. Retrieving it, she wondered again whatever made her buy it.

"But it suits you perfectly," the salesclerk had said. "With your figure and all that honey gold hair, the tangerine silk is a knockout. Your young man will be the envy of all his friends with you dressed like this."

There was no doubt the dress fit her perfectly, but the color was something Kathy had never tried before. She shook her head in disbelief at her own extravagance, trying to forget the price she'd paid for matching shoes.

As she entered the hotel, she glanced habitually toward the sky and noted a few scattered clouds. *Here comes that cold front Flight Service promised,* she thought and pushed open the door.

When Trevor finally arrived nearly a half hour late, Kathy breathed a sigh of relief, realizing how worried she'd really been. But her sigh was cut off sharply when she saw he wasn't alone.

"Kathy, I'd like you to meet Cynthia." Trevor smiled at her.

"She's darling, Trevie. She really is." A dark-haired woman stepped up beside him, draping herself on his arm.

Kathy's smile of welcome froze midway at the newcomer's tone. "Pleased, I'm sure," Kathy mumbled, stepping aside to follow them into the dining room.

She used the time to study Cynthia, noting her black, carefully curled hair that hung below her shoulders. She was probably near thirty, Kathy decided, although her flawless white skin made her seem younger.

And that dress, Kathy grimaced, looking down at her own casual pants, *must have come from New York.* The fuchsia slipdress was scooped deeply, revealing most of the woman's charms. And, Kathy noted, the way Trevor stared, he wasn't unaware of her beauty.

"Let's sit here," Cynthia slid her bare arm through Trevor's and drew him down beside her in a booth. Kathy sat alone opposite them, barely disguising her disgust.

"Is there something wrong, Kathy?" Trevor looked up at her after they'd ordered. "You haven't said a word since we got here."

"Maybe the cat's got her tongue, Trevie." Cynthia wrinkled her nose at him. "Maybe she's just not used to the big city!"

Kathy disregarded their comments. "I've ordered my food, and that's all I've needed to say," she stated coldly. "In fact, if I'm intruding on a private luncheon between you two, I can have the waiter serve mine at another table." She started to get up.

"Please sit down," Trevor sighed, a frown quickly replacing his smile. "We have things to discuss."

"Such as?" She kept her eyes on him, avoiding the smirk on Cynthia's face. Shocked at the intensity of her emotion, Kathy tried but couldn't formulate a reason for her feelings. She shouldn't care how Trevor acted with his girlfriend. But something unnamed deep inside her recoiled every time Cynthia touched him.

"Well, I thought you ought to know we'll be going out to Cynthia's from here. You can spend the afternoon with her, and then we'll all be dining this evening back here before we fly home."

"Trevie said you'd need some decent clothes for this evening," Cynthia purred, "and he thought I could find something . . . well, a bit more formal than what you're wearing." Her eyebrows rose to emphasize her meaning.

"If it's all the same to you, I'll just meet you here for dinner," Kathy ignored Cynthia and spoke to Trevor. "I'm sure I'd just be a bother to your . . . friend." She deliberately hesitated over that last word.

"But your clothes," Cynthia burst out. "You might be embarrassed dressed like that!" Her nose wrinkled in mock horror.

"I'll think of something," Kathy glared at the other woman, resting her arm on the dress box beside her.

Trevor glanced sharply from Kathy to Cynthia and back to Kathy. He opened his mouth to speak, but stopped when the waiter approached to place their food on the table.

By the time they had finished, Kathy couldn't remember exactly what she had eaten, or even *if* she'd eaten at all. But when Trevor escorted Cynthia out to his car and drove away with only a reminder that they had reservations for 7:30, she felt suddenly empty.

Kathy stormed to the telephones. *The first thing I'd better do,* she thought, *is get an update on the weather so I'll know how to plan for our flight this evening.*

The man in Flight Service answered her questions. "An isolated thunderstorm over Spokane, dissipating after midnight. But," he assured her, "the rest of the area between Spokane and Joseph is clear." She decided to delay their departure until late. That should give them an open flight home.

"Now," she muttered out loud, "it's time to change my image!" She walked across the lobby to the desk. Catching the eye of the desk clerk, she asked, "Is there a beauty shop near here?"

The clerk scribbled a phone number on a slip of paper while she carried on a conversation with a hotel guest through her headset.

Kathy phoned the shop and made an appointment. Then she hurried out into the beginnings of the storm, aiming for a department store. There were a few other things she'd need if she was going to wear her new dress.

On the way back, she was thankful for the covered skyways arching across Spokane's streets. While the rain pattered outside, she crossed from store to store in complete comfort. Once inside the beauty shop, Kathy felt cozy and secure and was pleased with the resulting hairstyle.

Taking advantage of a deserted ladies' lounge off the mezzanine of the hotel, Kathy prepared for the evening. "Lacey and her mom would be proud of me," she said at last, viewing the results of her afternoon efforts.

At ten minutes after seven, she stepped out wearing the

tangerine silk. Her golden hair was swept high off the nape of her neck, leaving a few delicate trailing tendrils.

Swishing softly as she slowly descended the stairs to the lobby, several men gave her an appreciative glance, but she barely noticed.

Her eyes focused on Trevor and Cynthia waiting below. When he looked up and caught sight of her, Trevor seemed to catch his breath as a strange look crossed his face. He let it out slowly as she approached.

"Where have you been?" he asked. "You left no message at the desk, and with the storm I—that is, we—were worried."

"Actually, I thought I was early." Kathy glanced at her watch. "Besides, I'm sure you've had plenty to do"—she glanced toward Cynthia and back to him—"to keep you from worrying too much."

Trevor shook his head slightly, but didn't comment. "Let's go upstairs," he said, leading the way to the elevators.

The ride to the rooftop restaurant was silent, but in the glare of the elevator light, Kathy took stock of her competition. *Competition? Now where did that word come from?* she mentally puzzled, dismissing her thoughts as she eyed Cynthia. The other woman's raven hair was a wavy cloud resting across her bare shoulders. Her wine satin gown superbly fitted over every curve, and the bodice—what there was of it—was outlined in rhinestones sweeping upward to form tiny straps against very white skin.

Trevor, she noted, had changed into a formal suit with a white shirt. Kathy tried not to think that he had changed at Cynthia's house, or even probably kept his clothes there, but she wasn't too successful.

Although she didn't feel outclassed, her own simple attempt at sophistication made her feel very young and inept. *If Trevor had to make a choice,* she thought sadly, *I know which one of us he would choose.*

As they stepped out of the elevator, Kathy deposited her packages with the desk attendant, not even attempting to analyze why she should think Trevor would need to make a choice. Instead, she followed him to a table by the window.

"Would anyone like a drink before dinner?" The waiter scanned their faces for a response.

"Just water, thank you," Kathy declared.

"I'll have coffee with mine," Trevor replied. The waiter disappeared when Cynthia just shook her head.

"I know Trevie never drinks anything stronger than coffee," Cynthia purred, "but why don't you? Too young?" She raised a plucked eyebrow in Kathy's direction.

"I don't need it." Kathy was grateful for her early Christian training. She was thankful that it had prevented her from developing harmful habits. "Some people need an artificial high, but I find other things are far more satisfying."

"Like flying, I presume?" Cynthia's purr had turned frosty. At Kathy's nod, she went on. "You're just like Trevie, everything he does centers around flying. The last time he flew—"

"Cynthia!" Trevor cut in sharply. "Kathy isn't interested in all this reminiscing."

"But I thought all pilots . . ." she stopped, pouting.

"What do you think of the view?" Trevor turned to smile at Kathy, blatantly ignoring Cynthia's pout. "The storm is nearly gone, and you can almost see the whole valley."

"It really is nice," Kathy admired the twinkling lights. "I'm glad you thought of eating here." She smiled broadly, enjoying the sulky look that clouded Cynthia's face. "By the way, speaking of flying, Flight Service indicated pretty good weather after midnight."

"You've already checked with them?" His tone showed approval.

"Uh-huh." She nodded. "We're all set for the return flight."

Thirty minutes into the new day, they were parked at the airport. In order to save time, Cynthia had gone home in a taxi and Kathy had changed back into her flying clothes. Trevor helped carry all her packages to the airplane while Kathy went to a telephone to file her flight plan.

"You're Kathy Evans?" the voice at Flight Service asked when she finished. "You have a message." He gave her a phone number in Joseph to call, mentioning that the message was marked urgent. Kathy dialed the number and was faintly surprised to recognize Jed's voice.

"Where the devil have you been?" he demanded. "I've been waiting for your call for hours."

"What's wrong?" Kathy chose not to explain. "Is there something wrong at home?"

"Of course not," he snapped. Then changing his tone, he said, "I'm sorry. It's been a long day, and I need a part for one of the engines I'm working on. It's an antique, and I finally located what I need in Spokane. When I tracked down your location, I hoped you could bring it back to me."

"I wish I could, but don't you think it's too late?" Kathy glanced at her watch, noting the hands had crept close to one o'clock. "I can't go banging on doors at this hour."

"You don't have to. Frank's at the airport now with the part. In fact, he said he'd wait near your plane so he wouldn't miss you. Just tell him who you are and that you want a package for Mr. James."

"Okay," she agreed, privately thinking it was a lot of fuss over an airplane part. "If I miss him, he'll just have to put it on the bus."

"Don't miss him," Jed stated firmly. "I need that package. And, Kathy," he added, "put it on my workbench when you get here. I'll leave the door unlocked."

She hung up and made her way back to the plane, thinking about Jed. In the three summers since she'd known him, he hadn't changed much. Except for the gruffness she'd noticed both last week and just now, he had the same carefree charm, mingled liberally with mechanic's grease. He was just Jed—every freckle, every red curl on his head, was the same.

Maybe, she thought, looking around for a parked car, *we'll get a chance to get to know each other better this summer.* She remembered Peggy's unfounded assumption that they would be getting married. Strangely, that idea didn't seem as exciting as it should. She wasn't sure she wanted to know why.

"What is this thing?" Trevor held up an odd-shaped package as she approached.

"It's a stuffed bear for my sister," she laughed at his quizzical look. "Peggy collects them, and I couldn't resist getting it for her. Lots of teenage girls go through a stuffed animal stage; Peggy's no exception."

"I'll take your word for it." He shook his head, stashing the bear in the backseat of the airplane. "Are we all set?"

"Not quite. I have to pick up a package. Oh, there he is . . ." Her voice trailed off as she spotted a man slowly walking toward them. Trevor didn't comment, but stayed close beside her as they approached the man in the shadows.

"Are you Frank?" Kathy asked. "Jed—that is, Mr. James—said you had a package for me."

The man only nodded and looked carefully from Kathy to Trevor and back again. He handed her a square box. "You'll see this gets to Mr. James right away?" His voice was low and gravelly.

"I'm flying directly there." Kathy felt a shiver run down her spine as she took the package. "I'll see that he gets it as soon as we land."

Apparently satisfied, the man turned on his heel and faded into the darkness.

"Friend of yours?" Trevor asked. Only then did Kathy realize he had placed his arm protectively around her shoulders. Cynthia or no Cynthia, for once she was glad to gather in the warmth and strength he offered.

"Never saw him before," she shuddered again. "Come on, let's get out of here."

6

While preparing for take-off, Kathy puzzled over the man she'd just met. If he was a friend of Jed's, then something was wrong somewhere. Although it was just an airplane part, Kathy's gut feeling told her something just wasn't right.

I'll try to see Jed tomorrow, she thought as she taxied onto the runway. *Whoever that guy was, I don't think Jed should have anything to do with him.* Airborne at last, Kathy began to relax after she switched on the autopilot.

"Look's like the storm is completely behind us. Nothing ahead but beautiful sky." She smiled at Trevor in the darkness. They both gazed at the velvet air sparkling with freshly washed stars.

"Tired?" Trevor asked. In the soft glow of the panel lights, his face, handsome as it was, took on such gentle, compassionate lines Kathy caught her breath.

"A little," she admitted. "Some strange guy got me up at the crack of dawn, and I've been going strong ever since."

"Careful," he chided with a smile, "there's no one here to protect you from that strange man now."

"Oh yes there is," she teased. "You wouldn't want to tangle with a giant bear, would you?"

"I surrender," he held up both hands mockingly. "Tell me about your sister—Peggy, did you say?"

"Actually, it's Margaret, but she doesn't want anyone to know. At sixteen, names are pretty important," Kathy shrugged. "Anyway, she's a bookworm and loves the ocean." Kathy corrected her heading by five degrees.

"Does she fly too?"

"No. She and Mom say two pilots in the family is enough. I imagine she'll end up teaching literature or something along that line."

"Sounds logical." Trevor shrugged and turned slightly toward Kathy in his seat.

Kathy caught him doing it again—talking to her, but methodically scanning her instrument panel at the same time. *Sort of like my Flight Instructor used to do,* she mused silently.

"And what does the future hold for Peggy's sister?" She almost missed his soft question.

"I don't know right now," she shook her head slowly. The intimacy of a night-wrapped cockpit made the question very normal. "I guess I'll fly for Dad until Prince Charming comes along—or Dad gets tired of me, whichever comes first. Then, I suppose I'll have to fall back on my business degree."

She didn't mention how often she had prayed about that very thing. It was so hard to answer his question with an "I don't know." Kathy thought of all the kids at school, the ones who'd known so clearly where their paths would lead. Her own roommate was already in an executive position, and her best friend was going on to graduate school.

But what about me, God? Kathy lifted a silent prayer. *Where do I fit? What am I supposed to be doing?*

They flew silently through the night. Kathy tried to picture Jed as Prince Charming, but every time he tried to mount his white horse, he got grease all over the saddle. She sighed unconsciously.

"Something wrong?" Trevor broke into her thoughts. "Perhaps I've asked too much of you today."

"No, I'm fine, really. It's just something I'm puzzling

over," she assured him, scanning the panel again. She looked up to smile and caught the tail end of his scan, too.

"Anything I can help with?"

"No," she shook her head, wondering why it was so easy to picture Trevor sitting on a prancing white horse.

The night deepened, wrapping them in its intimate blanket of isolation. Their mood and movements meshed so gently, Kathy hardly noticed their landing and the shift to the car where Trevor took over control.

When at last the pillow claimed her head, Kathy's final thoughts were of Trevor's intense blue eyes. "I wish it could always be like this," she whispered into the folds of her pillow.

———

Kathy stretched lazily and rolled over. Slowly, the awareness of the strange room caused her to cautiously open her eyes. The soft light seeping around the cream drapes cast a gentle illumination in the old-fashioned bedroom. A smile tweaked the corners of her mouth as she searched for her watch.

"Almost noon," she murmured. "I'm not surprised." Getting out of bed, she opened the drapes to allow the full noon sun to flood her room. Scenes from the previous night dominated her thoughts as she prepared to meet the day.

When Trevor had offered to deliver Jed's package into the unlocked but darkened mechanic's shop, Kathy had been only too glad to let him do it.

"I'm usually not afraid of the dark," she muttered, brushing her golden hair to a sheen, "but last night was almost unreal. Must have been that creepy Frank that started it all. He seemed so strange."

The more she thought about it, the more sure she was she needed to have a talk with Jed as soon as possible. *Next time,* she thought, *he can have his airplane parts delivered by bus!*

Only one other thing bothered her as she stepped into the claw-footed tub and pulled the curtain for a shower. The memory of Trevor's arm around her sent a quick flush to her cheeks. True, he'd meant it only as a protection, but in spite of the situation a warm tingle had run through her veins. She'd never felt that way with Jed.

"Comfortable," she murmured, reaching for the faucet, "but not tingling—Whoa!" She gasped as a blast of cold water brought her back to reality.

Although she wasn't ready for lunch, Kathy put together a fruit salad and toast. Outside it looked like a good day to wander around the campgrounds if Trevor didn't need her.

She finished her salad and rinsed out her dishes. She then spent a quiet half hour with her usual daily devotions, ending with a prayer for a better, more stable relationship with her employer. Finally she sauntered across the porch and knocked on Trevor's camper door to see if he had plans. When there was no response, she wrote a short note telling him she'd be back in an hour, and taped it to the door.

Warm dust raised in little puffs around her feet as she ambled along the deeply rutted lane. There were children playing along the road everywhere. They darted among the trees and rushed from cabins to campers. But the animals caught Kathy's attention most. There were dogs, squirrels, and even a few tame deer.

She stopped to watch a little boy feeding some marshmallows to a doe. She didn't know which one ate more, the boy or the doe. But they both looked as though they were enjoying the sweet, sticky treat.

Around the bend, she caught sight of the church camp and decided to drop in on Professor Strauss.

The fence and gate were made of rustic poles lashed together, blending perfectly with the park surroundings.

Turning in at the gate, she soon found him sitting in the shade of a large old tree.

"Got a minute to spare for a friend?" Kathy hailed him as she plopped down on the lush grass.

"You're certainly welcome." Professor Strauss shifted his Bible off his lap. "But what are you doing here?"

"I hope I'm not interrupting something important?"

"No. I'm just going over some notes for this evening's chapel session." He turned gentle eyes on her. "Now, what's up?"

"I'm here on a charter. In fact, it's sort of a strange situation." Kathy crossed her jean-clad legs. Then, with an easiness she couldn't explain, she began to pour out the whole thing to him.

After she told him her story, Professor Strauss drew one knee up and rested his arms around it. "Kathy, I know it may sound a bit strange, but your dad doesn't seem like the kind of person who would knowingly send you into a bad situation. I'm sure he's checked out this Mr. Kingston thoroughly."

"I know. I trust Dad's judgment too." Kathy picked up a fallen pinecone and turned it over and over. "I suppose everything's okay. It's just such an unusual situation, and I feel a bit off-balance with Trevor—that is, Mr. Kingston." She stumbled over his name and unconsciously jabbed the air with the pinecone as if to emphasize her point.

Professor Strauss nodded at her. "Now, tell me, how are you handling your other questions?" He shifted to face her squarely. "The last time we talked you were wondering what you should be doing with your life."

"I'm trying to take it a day at a time. But sometimes I get discouraged thinking about some of my friends who know exactly what they're supposed to be doing."

"Could that be your problem?"

"What?"

"You're trying to figure it out on your own." Professor Strauss tapped his Bible. "Your dad is a praying man; he must have taught you to pray too. Have you asked God for guidance?"

"Actually, I have," she smiled at his careful question. "I've been a Christian for a long time," she assured him, "but sometimes it seems very difficult to know exactly where God is leading me."

"In that case," he returned her smile, "you're in very good hands. Be patient and wait. Let God choose what you are to do, and then allow Him to work through you."

"You sound a lot like my dad," she gave a nervous laugh and stood up. "But I've got to get back." Kathy glanced at her watch. "I left a note for Trevor, and I'm almost late now."

"So now it's Trevor," he teased. "A few minutes ago it was Mr. Kingston."

"Oh no. It's nothing like that," Kathy protested. "He just told me to call him Trevor."

They walked back toward the gate together. "Will you pray seriously for God to show you His plan for your life? Remember, it may take a while for Him to answer." Professor Strauss stopped at the gate.

"I will," Kathy promised, pushing open the rails and stepping through. "And may I come visit you again? It helps me to sort things out."

"You know you're always welcome."

She waved and hurried back to the cabin. When she reached the camper, she called through the closed screen door, "Will you be needing me this afternoon?"

"Did you have something special in mind?" Trevor sauntered to the screen, but didn't open it.

"Just thought I might go out to the airport," Kathy shrugged. "I'd like to talk to Jed—"

"Oh yes, your *friend*." Trevor pulled back into the shadows of the camper, his voice sharper than she remembered. "I suppose you want to borrow my car too."

"I could walk," Kathy retorted, then was instantly sorry she'd let her temper flare.

"Here," he pushed the screen open slightly and thrust the keys at her. "Just don't be gone long. I never know what may come up."

"I promise I won't go anywhere else," Kathy lightened the mood by mimicking a teen's response to a dominating parent. "You can reach me at the airport if something important happens."

As she drove away from the cabin, her mind quickly shifted to Jed and her mounting feeling that she needed to talk to him very seriously. Although mindful of the vacationers, Kathy hardly noticed them as she drove through the park. Even the little pond at the park's entrance with its enormous pet fish didn't catch her attention today.

I hope Jed's at the shop. The sudden thought brought her up short. *I should have called to be sure.* For once, the sight of Jed's battered pickup brought a reluctant sigh to her lips. As much as she cared for him, she was dreading this meeting. She pulled in beside the pickup and turned off the car. She glanced at her plane tethered docilely beside the others. The frown on her forehead softened slightly as she thought about the past night's flight home.

"Jed, are you in here?" Kathy poked her head into the shop, but couldn't see anyone.

"Kathy?" Jed's voice sounded muffled. "Over here—inside the Maule."

Kathy picked her way across the tool-strewn floor to where Jed's feet were visible under a black and red Maule. His head and shoulders were completely swallowed inside the tail section. Wriggling backward, he slid to the outside.

"What's up?" He glanced at her, then turned to retrieve a screwdriver.

"Did you find your package okay?" That was the best place to start, Kathy thought.

"Oh yeah, thanks," Jed muttered, not looking at her. "It was just what I needed."

"That guy, Frank—the one in Spokane?" Kathy hedged a bit, then hit it straight on. "I don't like him."

"Who? Frank?" Jed straightened up, cocking an eyebrow at her. "What difference does it make?" He shrugged. "Besides, how can you form an opinion so fast?"

"I just know these things," Kathy leaned against the strut as Jed gathered up his tools. "Deep in the pit of my stomach I know something's wrong with that guy, and I don't think you should have anything to do with him."

"Listen to the little brat telling me what to do!" Jed threw his tools helter-skelter in a box and tossed a grease rag in a barrel.

"I'm not a little brat—at least not anymore!" Kathy didn't like his tone, but decided he must be teasing her.

"Yeah, I noticed." Jed scribbled on a piece of paper with a stubby pencil. "Since you're all educated now, I should have *you* doing this paper work instead of me."

"No way," she protested, "Dad's got me doing enough of that in Pendleton."

Not satisfied with his brush-off, Kathy tried again. "How did you find me last night anyway?"

"Saw your plane here late the night before and called Flight Service." Jed threw down the pencil and pushed the paper off to one side of the messy counter. "You always did file a flight plan. That makes it easy."

"I should have thought of that. Want some coffee?" Kathy took a step toward the office.

"No thanks, I gotta keep working on that Maule. The owner wants it ready by late afternoon, and it's almost done."

"I mean it, Jed." Kathy followed him back to the airplane. "About Frank, that is. I really don't think you should have anything to do with him. He gives me the creeps!"

"Women!" Jed raised his hands in mock despair. "Spare me! The guy's not so bad once you get to know him. Besides"—he turned an unusually harsh glare on her—"I'll pick my own friends without any help from you. You're just a kid."

"Do what you want about your *friends*, but I'll thank you to remember that I'm not just a kid. You said so yourself."

"Oh yeah, all grown up now," he ran his eyes over her as if for the first time. "You're a little more filled out here and there, but you're still as pesky as ever." He smiled to break the strain between them, but the smile didn't quite reach his eyes.

"Pesky! Is that what you think of me?" Kathy's temper rose. "When I think of all the times I've tagged after you, helped you work on planes, written to you—"

"Hold it! Of course I thought you were pesky—but a nice pesky, or I wouldn't have let you hang around. Like now, for instance." Jed knelt down by the toolbox and selected a wrench. "Most other mechanics I know wouldn't put up with a woman pestering them while they're working. But I don't mind. You've always been useful."

"Useful!" Kathy felt unwelcome tears spring to her eyes. "But I thought we were friends, even good friends."

"We *are* friends." Jed stuck his head through the baggage door of the Maule. "Now be a good friend and bring me some paper towels. They're on the shelf by the door."

Fetch and carry! Kathy fumed softly as she picked her way across the floor. *And Peggy thought—I thought—there was so much more.*

She paused by the door, tempted to tell him to get his own paper towels, but couldn't quite do it. She could see that Jed was really busy.

"Maybe that's it," she wondered out loud as she opened

the door to Trevor's car after saying goodbye. "Jed was busy, and my timing was all wrong. Or maybe I'm trying to push our friendship beyond where he wants it to go." Confused, Kathy drove back to the cabin, more uncertain than ever about Jed.

7

$\mathcal{E}$vening shadows traced long fingers across the valley as Kathy rinsed out her supper dishes and hung up the dish towel to dry. She grabbed a jacket and a couple pillows and sauntered out to the patio. Trevor was nowhere to be seen; he hadn't answered her knock when she returned the car keys, but she had heard his car back out of the driveway later that afternoon.

She'd just settled down to watch some deer ambling down the path to the river when the quiet was shattered by the ringing telephone. Expecting Trevor's voice, she stuttered a bit when she heard her mother's gentle "How are you, dear?" Before she could respond, her mother launched into the latest news.

"By the way," her mom finally slowed down after describing Peggy's most recent escapade, "you are planning to attend Kurt's wedding on Saturday, aren't you? I mean, it just wouldn't be right for you not to go."

"Actually, Mom," Kathy stifled a groan. "I had forgotten it. Things have been so scrambled this summer, I haven't given it a single thought."

"I was afraid of that," her mother countered quickly. "I suppose you haven't picked out a dress or made arrangements to get away from your job either."

"As usual, you're right." Kathy grinned—her mother knew her too well. "Mr. Kingston isn't here right now, but as soon as he returns I'll check with him. I'm fairly sure there won't be a problem, but with him I just never know."

"What do you mean, dear? Is he difficult?"

"Not really," Kathy tried to explain, "it's just that he's unpredictable. One moment he'll be gracious and understanding, but then the next he'll turn a complete about-face and be as obstinate as grandpa's mule. There's just no way to be sure."

"Treat him with kindness," her mother advised with a laugh. "I can't think of a mule or a man who could resist your smile! In the meantime, I'll pray about it, and so can you."

"I love you, Mom," Kathy ended the call. "Give Dad and Peggy big hugs too."

Out on the patio again, Kathy snuggled into the pillows as twilight deepened into a soft summer night. The stars came into view and a soft sighing whispered in the tips of the trees.

"Kurt," she mused aloud. "I haven't seen him in years, and now he's getting married. I just can't believe it."

"Another boyfriend bit the dust, huh?" Trevor's voice drifted across the patio from the darkness of his camper.

Kathy jerked upright, startled. She hadn't noticed that the car was back in its place. He must have come home while she was on the phone.

"Sorry to disappoint you," Kathy dripped sweetness, remembering her mother's advice, "but Kurt is my cousin, not a boyfriend."

Trevor stepped out of the shadows into the soft gray light of the moon and stars. "My mistake," he shrugged as he eased into a lounge chair near her, "but with you, I never know."

Kathy almost choked as she heard him use words to describe her that she had used for him. "Apparently there's a lot we don't know about each other," she countered softly.

Quietness settled around them. In the underbrush,

crickets chirped in syncopated rhythm, broken by occas-
sional muffled footfalls on the animal trails. At last Kathy
stirred in the pillows and murmured across the darkness.
"Trevor, about the wedding . . . my mom really wants me
to go with the family. Would you mind terribly if I took a
day or two off?"

"If it's something you really want to do," his tone
matched her own, "of course you can have whatever time
you need. When?"

Kathy smiled at his response—her mother's prayers
must be very powerful. "The wedding's not until Saturday,
but Mom reminded me that I'll need to get a dress, I haven't
a—"

"A thing to wear," he finished for her with a laugh. "I've
heard that line before."

"But it's true," she protested, sitting up straight in the
chair.

"You couldn't possibly wear that devastating dress you
had on at dinner in Spokane," he mocked her slightly.

"It's not appropriate," she stammered, shocked at the
idea that he had paid any attention at all to what she'd been
wearing that night, let alone thought it was devastating.

"It was appropriate *then*," he replied. "But I suppose
you know best." He stood up and stretched. "Weddings
never really interested me that much. Go and do whatever
you need to do, but don't forget to come back."

Kathy stood up, too, and caught just a glimpse of the
look on his face as he said that last phrase. If she hadn't
known better, it almost looked pleading. Once more remembering her mother's advice, she turned so the moonlight glinted on her face and gave him a great big smile.

"Thanks, you're really wonderful to let me have the time
off on such short notice." Kathy felt relief bubble inside her.
"My mother thanks you," she laughed, "my sister thanks
you—and, of course, my cousin thanks you."

She twirled and playfully tossed a pillow at him. "And I'll be back just as soon as Kurt says 'I do.' "

———————

The next morning Kathy landed at the Pendleton Airport, checked at the office for her absent father, and drove home. Peggy was the only one to greet her.

"Mom drove to Walla Walla to help Rachel and Terry get ready for the reception. They're going to hold it in their backyard by the pool." Peggy followed Kathy to her bedroom and flopped on the bed. "Terry told Mom he'd waited so long for his brother to get married he'd do anything to help." Peggy rolled over on her back and watched Kathy methodically search through her closet. "I got to see their baby last week. He's so cute!"

"Baby?" Kathy stopped suddenly with her hand on a green dress. "Whose baby?"

"Terry and Rachel's, of course." Peggy rattled on, "Don't you remember she had a little boy last Thanksgiving?"

"I wasn't here." Kathy returned to sliding hangers, slowly considering then rejecting each outfit. "I was in college, remember?"

"They wanted to name him Kurt after his new uncle," Peggy continued, "but Jenny said she hoped to have a little boy someday and wanted to keep that name for him. They named him Seth after Rachel's dad. I just love that name!"

"You just love babies," Kathy shook her head. "And I have absolutely nothing to wear!" she sighed.

"I know," Peggy giggled. "I already looked through your closet!"

"Typical sister." Kathy playfully cuffed her sister on the arm. "Well, since you and I both agree, do you have any wonderful suggestions? There really isn't time to make anything." She thought of the tangerine silk hanging in her closet at the lake and was glad Peggy didn't know about it. With her dramatic flare, Peggy would insist that it was perfect.

"What about Lacey's dress shop?" Peggy sat up on the bed so she could see her reflection in the dresser mirror. She immediately tugged the scrunchie out of her hair, pulled the whole mass up and into a relaxed style.

"It's a good thing you're a teenager," Kathy laughed. "Only the young can get away with that hairstyle. And you're right, let's go to Lacey's."

"I can go with you?" Peggy stood up and cocked her head in question.

"Of course." Kathy gave her sister a quick hug. "I need your opinion. Can't risk showing up in something horrible. You're the fashion expert, aren't you?"

The sisters piled into Kathy's car and drove to the dress shop. Kathy glanced at Peggy and smiled softly. *She really is growing up,* she thought. *I think I like who she's becoming.*

Lacey's mother met them at the door. "I just knew you'd show up this week," she beamed at Kathy. "When your mother told me about your cousin's wedding, I started picking out some special dresses just for you." She drew them past Lacey, who was waiting on another customer, and into the back room, where she scooped up an armload of bright dresses.

"Get started on these." She handed them to Kathy and pointed her toward the dressing room. "I may have a couple more options, if you don't find what you want there. But pay special attention to the green one."

Kathy laughed as she closed the door. Lacey's mother always saved the "green one" for her.

"Married, who's getting married?" Lacey's voice carried through the closed door when she finished with her customer.

"Our cousin Kurt." Peggy answered. "It's just so romantic! She took flying lessons from him, and they fell in love. Isn't that great?"

"When did all this happen," Lacey tapped on the dressing-room door. "I mean, wasn't he the old bachelor cousin you were always talking about?"

Kathy stepped out into the room wearing a pink floral dress with a scooped neck. "We'd all given up on Kurt. I thought he'd never get married." She pivoted in front of the mirror and shook her head.

"It happened last summer," Peggy poured out the details while Kathy tried on another dress. "They were planning a Christmas wedding because Jenny—that's her name—moved to Walla Walla from Seattle and started an art gallery. Kurt built it for her at the airport. She wanted to get everything settled before they got married."

"An art gallery?" Lacey shook her head at the yellow dress Kathy held up. "Not you at all!" she whispered.

"Uh-huh," Peggy nodded. "She calls it Mountain Art because his business is called Mountain Sky. Anyway"—Peggy pursed her lips thoughtfully at the navy-and-white suit Kathy was now wearing—"Anyway, they didn't get married at Christmas because she got sick the week before the wedding—I think it was the flu. Then in January she ended up in the hospital with pneumonia. The doctor said it was because she was so run-down from working at the art gallery and getting ready for the wedding."

Kathy thought the navy suit would do, but decided to try the green dress just to make Lacey's mom happy. It looked so plain on the hanger.

"But that was in January," Lacey prompted Peggy. "This is June. What took so long?"

"She was awfully sick. Mom said she was in bed for four months! That's the worst thing I can think of—doing absolutely nothing for four months!" Peggy sauntered over to the jewelry case and held up some long, dangly earrings with brightly colored glass. "By the time she got well, it was nearly June, so Jenny decided to wait and have it this month. She's always wanted a June wedding."

"Try the little gold hoops." Lacey gently guided Peggy away from the garish earrings. "With your hair pulled up away from your face, those hoops would look absolutely elegant."

"Speaking of elegant . . ." Kathy stepped out into the room once again, this time wearing the green dress. "This is wonderful. How did you know?" She smiled at Lacey's mom. "I thought the dress was far too plain the way it looked on the hanger."

"The dress wasn't designed for the hanger," Lacey and her mom both spoke at once.

"It brings out the color of your eyes, not to mention what it does for your figure!" Lacey raised an approving eyebrow. "Besides, it's so basic, you can do lots of changes. Come over here and I'll show you." She led Kathy to a counter piled with scarfs and jewelry. For the next half hour the girls played with belts and jackets, pins and scarfs.

"Enough!" Kathy finally held up her hands in surrender. "I feel like an overgrown Barbie doll. I'll take the dress!" As soon as she'd said it, an unbidden thought raced through her mind. *I wonder if Trevor would like it?* Somehow she thought he would, but she doubted if he'd call it *devastating*.

By late afternoon their mother had returned home. All three were talking about the wedding while they cooked supper. None of them were prepared for the ashen look on their father's face when he came through the door.

"Dad," Kathy reacted first when she saw him. "What's wrong?" She wiped her hands on her apron and pulled out a chair for him. All three women clustered around him as he sank gratefully into the chair.

"Once again, God has answered our prayers." He

reached out and grasped his wife's hand. "It was so close, so very close."

Puzzled, Kathy watched a look of deep understanding pass between her parents. "What was close, Dad?"

"A student turned the wrong way just as I was entering the pattern," he shook his head and pursed his lips. "He pulled up underneath me—you know that blind spot just as you make the turn?" He looked at Kathy.

She nodded, waiting for her sister's inevitable outburst. For once Peggy said absolutely nothing. Kathy noticed the silence and stole a quick glance at both her mother and sister. Their reaction was the same. *Two peas in a pod*, Kathy thought. *White around the eyes and knuckles.*

"Is he hurt?" their mother finally asked in a tiny voice.

"Didn't even scrape the aircrafts," he answered, once again shaking his head. "Only the width of an angel's wing kept us apart. But if I'm this badly shaken, can you imagine how he must feel!"

"For he will command his angels concerning you to guard you in all your ways," their mother quoted the familiar scripture while leaning over her husband. She gave him a gentle hug. "I'm so glad we pray for God's protection every day. With you and Kathy in the air so much of the time, I wouldn't have a minute's peace if I didn't trust God to take care of you."

"Praying doesn't mean we won't have an accident." Her father took a deep breath and reached out for Kathy's hand. "But we can praise God when He intervenes on our behalf. A hundred things could have gone wrong just at that moment, and neither of us would be alive right now."

Kathy heard her dad continue as her parents moved into the living room. "They're so young, so vulnerable," he said. "They just don't realize how unforgiving flying can be. One moment of inattention, one second of hesitation, and disaster comes crashing to earth!"

It was at that point that Kathy realized her father was not telling the whole story. He never unnecessarily worried his wife or family. His obviously shaken attitude told her a whole lot more had happened. *In fact,* she thought to herself, *he might not even tell* me *the whole story.* But if it shook her father that much, she was glad God had chosen to protect him.

———————

Saturday morning dawned bright and beautiful. As the family drove the forty-five-mile distance from Pendleton across the Washington state line to Walla Walla, Kathy couldn't help but notice the tenderness her parents showed to each other in the front seat.

"What's with you two this morning?" she teased them. "You act like this is *your* wedding instead of Kurt's."

"In a way it *is* ours." Her father lifted her mother's hand and gently brushed her wedding ring with his lips. It was such a romantic act, Kathy was almost embarrassed. "You see, every wedding we attend, your mother and I quietly renew our vows along with the bride and groom. It's just something we've always done. It's a great reminder of the vows we took all those years ago."

"There have been a couple of times"—her mother glanced in the backseat at the two girls—"when it was very important in our marriage to renew those vows. Even for Christians marriage can be tough. We need to be reminded that God is the One who holds us together."

Peggy opened the car door as soon as they stopped. She sped toward the backyard and was soon fully engrossed in playing with the baby.

Kathy helped her mother and Rachel lay out the silver and napkins as soon as her father and Terry had set up the tables. She glanced at the sky and noticed once again how clear it was. "Looks like we won't have to worry about rain today," she commented to Rachel.

"I was really concerned when it rained last night." Rachel followed her gaze and nodded. "But Terry promised that it would be clear today. With his job working with weather reports at Flight Service, sometimes he forgets God is more in control of the weather than he is!"

"I heard that!" Terry walked up behind his wife and tugged her hair playfully before giving her a hug. "God and I work together—He makes the weather, and I report it!"

"I'm just glad the sun is shining." Kathy smiled at her cousin and his wife. "Nothing's too good for Kurt and Jenny's wedding day."

8

Kathy smoothed her green skirt underneath her as she slid into the church pew between her mother and Peggy. As far as she could remember she had never attended any function in this particular church. "Lovely," she murmured to Peggy as she took a slow, sweeping view of the sanctuary. The entire chancel wall was white brick dominated by a single towering cross and sidelighted by a column of opaque stained glass on each end. Blond pews and twice-high arching beams added a lifting, cloudlike atmosphere.

"Aren't the decorations wonderful?" Peggy whispered, her eyes glistening in the candlelit softness.

Kathy was startled to realize she had not even noticed the wedding decorations while she was admiring the church. Now she followed Peggy's lead and nodded agreement.

The decor was simple, yet elegant. Two slender white tapers rested on a satin-draped altar table at the foot of the cross on either side of a thick white wedding candle. The kneeling board in front of the altar, also draped in white satin, was flanked by two tall white wicker baskets filled with luscious banks of trailing ivy. At each side of the platform was a swirled stand of green candles. Green and white bows decorated the pews. The organist changed songs, and Kathy watched her aunt and uncle being ushered up the aisle.

"Mom said they just got here yesterday," Peggy whispered.

71

Both girls strained slightly to glimpse Kurt's parents. They hadn't seen them since their last missionary furlough from Indonesia five years ago. "They almost look the same," Kathy noted. "Hardly changed at all."

"I always thought it was glamorous the way they decided to become missionaries after Kurt and Terry grew up."

On the other side of the church, an older woman was being escorted down the aisle to the traditional mother-of-the-bride seat. "Is that Jenny's mother?" Kathy nudged her mother.

"No, it's her housekeeper. I believe Rachel said Jenny's parents aren't living." Her mother smiled and squeezed Kathy's hand. "I understand they are very close."

A door opened just beyond the organ, and a young minister with dark hair stepped into the room followed by Kurt, Terry, and another young man Kathy couldn't see very well. It had been a long time since she had seen Kurt. He was a taller, older version of Terry with thick blond hair. All the men wore dark tuxedos with forest green ties and cummerbunds. Kurt's lapel was graced with a white rose and a sprig of ivy.

As the men turned to face the audience, Kathy gasped out loud. "It's Professor Strauss!" Embarrassed, she ducked her head.

"Someone you know, dear?" Her mother's soft voice had a calming effect.

"He was a charter earlier this summer. I've had a chance to talk with him up at the lake." Kathy slowly regained her composure. "What's he doing here?"

"I think he was in school with the boys—a college roommate of Kurt's his last year, if I remember what Rachel and Terry said."

The music switched again, this time to the traditional bridesmaid's theme.

On the other side of the church, Kathy could see a slender young lady walking down the aisle. Her long dark hair was caught at the crown with a puff of white lace and a spray of ivy. She wore a deep green tea-length gown and carried a bouquet of three white roses draped in ivy.

"Must be someone from Seattle," Peggy commented. "I've never seen her around here."

When she was halfway down the long aisle, Rachel came through the door in an identical gown. Both young women moved slowly to the front of the church and took their places.

The older woman who was acting as mother of the bride stood, and the music swelled into the traditional wedding march. The audience rose and turned to face the bride. Kathy couldn't see through all the crowd, so she had to wait until the bride and an older man escorting her reached the front.

"She's so tiny," Peggy murmured under cover of the music.

"Just the kind of girl I'd expect Kurt to choose," Kathy whispered when she finally saw Jenny.

Beneath a shoulder-length white lace veil crested with pearls, dark curls frothed around her beaming face as the bride glanced toward Kurt. The bodice of her traditional floor-length satin gown was touched with pearls and sequins that sparkled in the candlelight. A graceful sweep of ivy and white roses with one rose tipped in a blush of pink right in the center rested on her arm.

Kathy pulled her attention back to the ceremony. The bride was now moving toward the center of the room to take her place beside Kurt.

"Dearly beloved," the pastor spoke the familiar words. "We are gathered together here in the sight of God, and in the presence of these witnesses, to join together this man and this woman in holy matrimony, which is an honorable estate, instituted by God. It is, therefore, not to be entered into unadvisedly, but reverently, discreetly, and in the fear of God."

Kathy felt a movement beside her and turned slightly. She saw her father reach out and grasp her mother's hand. For just a moment, Kathy sensed an exclusion, as though the only two people in her parents' lives at that moment were themselves. A tiny lump caught in her throat at the tenderness on their faces.

As the ceremony continued, the bride and groom knelt at the foot of the cross and bowed their heads. Dr. Strauss turned to face the audience as the organ pealed the first notes of a wedding song. Kathy had never heard him sing and wondered what it would be like.

His deep voice poured into the room, filling the sanctuary. "It's only God's love," he sang with his eyes lifted above the crowd, "that brings fulfillment. It's only God's love that brings true joy." The music was soft and prayerful. He brought the melody to a close. "Two hearts, united in God's love, will last for a lifetime." As he turned back to face the bride and groom, Kathy was convinced that he really meant those words.

As she bowed her head for the prayer, Kathy was sure that God cared very much about her and who she might marry. Part of her restless wondering about the future eased slightly in that moment. She was so lost in thought that Peggy nudged her at the end of the prayer.

"Are you okay?" she whispered. "You looked as if you were asleep."

"I'm fine," Kathy answered. "Just thinking, that's all." She tuned back in to what the pastor was saying.

"It was just about a year ago that I first saw Kurt bring this lovely woman into our church." He glanced at the two of them as they stood in front of him. "And from the look on Kurt's face, I knew exactly what his intentions were." He grinned at Kurt, who squirmed slightly. "My wife says I can smell a wedding long before the bride and groom ever know it—and I sure smelled one that morning."

Kathy watched the lighthearted interplay going on between the pastor and her cousin. Here was a relationship with a pastor that spoke of real caring, real understanding. This man truly cared about Kurt and Jenny.

"We've been through a lot of good times and some not so great times together this past year. But through it all, I have found both Kurt and Jenny to be people who not only have a growing love for each other, but a growing love for God. I can't think of a better foundation for a marriage than loving God."

Kathy listened intently, sitting slightly forward on the pew. *I wonder what Trevor would think about this wedding,* she pondered silently. His comment about weddings not meaning much to him almost seemed out of character.

The pastor continued. "Right now things look wonderful for you. It's June and you are beautiful and young and in love.

"But one of these days it's going to be December, and you won't be so young anymore. There will be wrinkles and gray hair and even heartache, and you won't be quite so sure you love your spouse. That's when candlelight and satin and lace won't have much meaning. You won't be remembering your wedding then.

"But by the grace of God's love," he smiled gently at them, "you *can* be thinking marriage. When a marriage is formed and bonded in God's love from the very beginning, God's love will keep it together and pull it through the tough times when human love isn't enough."

Kathy remembered her parents' conversation in the car that morning. She turned slightly and caught her father in the act of brushing her mother's wedding ring with a gentle touch.

A few moments later, after their vows had been spoken,

Kathy watched Kurt lift Jenny's veil and draw her into a tender kiss.

"It gives me the utmost pleasure," the pastor said when the kiss ended and the new couple turned to face the audience, "to introduce to you for the very first time, Mr. and Mrs. Kurt and Jenny Adams."

The music swelled into the recessional as the bridal party swept down from the altar and out the aisle. As Kurt and Jenny passed near her, Kathy saw radiant joy on their faces.

Just for a moment, she imagined that she was the bride—but she couldn't picture Jed in Kurt's place. The vows were too serious, too deeply connected to God's love, for the Jed she knew. Yet she could easily imagine Trevor standing beside her. She quickly shook off the thought, wondering what those vows would mean to him . . . and to Cynthia.

At the reception, Kathy was introduced to Maggie, Jenny's housekeeper. She liked her instantly and saw the obvious love that flowed between the two women. Then she met Sandy, the bridesmaid with the long dark hair. Sandy, it turned out, had worked for Jenny in Seattle and now worked in Jenny's art gallery at the airport.

"And this is my little cousin Kathy." Kurt drew his bride up beside her. "Who obviously isn't so little anymore," he whistled softly.

"Hey"—Jenny playfully poked him—"those whistles are only for me from now on. Hi, Kathy." She stretched out a hand. "Don't mind him. I'm delighted to meet you."

Kathy saw the genuine interest in Jenny's eyes. "I always wondered who would ever have the courage to take on my cousin," she responded cheerfully. "But I can see you'll keep him in line just fine. I can't wait to get to know you better. I have so many great little stories to tell you about him."

Kurt gave her shoulders a gentle hug. "Now listen, Kathy, there'll be none of that. This woman thinks I'm wonderful, and I won't have you spoiling my image!"

Kathy watched them swirl through the crowd, meeting people and thoroughly enjoying the whole thing. "Now there's a couple who's going to make it," she murmured to herself.

"I agree with you." A familiar voice spoke in her ear. Kathy whirled around and came nose-to-nose with Dr. Strauss. "I believe they'll make it. They're in love with each other, but they both really love God too."

"I had no idea you knew my cousin," Kathy said.

"He's a great guy and a terrific Christian. I don't know what took him so long to bite the dust, though." Dr. Strauss shook his head in wonder, "He had girls standing in line waiting for him at college, but he never even gave them a glance."

"Seems to me if you were his roommate, you're taking a bit of time yourself," Kathy countered, caught up in all the wedding talk.

"Actually, there is someone," he grinned. "We plan to announce our engagement in the fall and hope to be married next summer after she graduates from college. Her parents really want her to finish school first."

"Congratulations." Kathy raised her punch glass in a toast. They drifted apart and Kathy moved to her mother's side.

She stopped at the edge of the pool and caught a glimpse of the afternoon sun's rays reflected there. All around the pool was noise and motion, but the water was still. *That's what I need,* she thought. *My mind and thoughts are spinning everywhere—what I really need is to be still.*

"Peace be still." An inner voice brought a Bible verse to her mind. She pictured a boat filled with terrified disciples and the figure of Jesus standing with outstretched arms.

"Peace be still," He had said, and the wind and the waves had obeyed Him.

I wish my mind would calm that quickly, she thought. *Some peace would be wonderful.* Instantly her mind was filled with a picture of Trevor's face the way she'd seen it that night when she told him about coming to the wedding. *I think he needs some peace too,* she thought.

Suddenly she realized that she'd been thinking about Trevor all day, wondering what he'd think about the wedding or how he'd feel. Although there was a slight tension between them, there was already a bond. Right now Kathy missed him.

Hours later when they'd all thrown rice at Kurt and Jenny as they taxied their airplane out on the first leg of their honeymoon trip to Hawaii, Kathy realized it was time to go home. But she wasn't thinking of Pendleton and her family, she was thinking of Trevor and Wallowa Lake.

9

A week slipped by with Trevor keeping busy in his camper. When they were together, he was always polite, but distant in a preoccupied sort of way. Even the Fourth of July holiday with its wonderful fireworks display and giant swell of vacationers did little to improve their relationship.

But as the days after the wedding wore quietly on, Kathy's tension relaxed. Although she wanted to go home, Trevor never once suggested that she return to her father and normal business.

She drove again to the airport to visit with Jed, but he was so busy she didn't stay long. Slowly she drifted into a vacation routine. There were lovely long walks in the early morning along pretty trails. In the afternoon she spent lazy hours in the sun reading a book or writing letters.

One Saturday late in July, they took what had become a weekly routine flight to La Grande and back. Both times Trevor requested they fly directly over the Minam Horse Ranch. Kathy assumed it gave him some small sense of security.

This time when they got back and she had tied down the plane, Kathy decided to stay and talk some more with Jed. Her uneasiness had given way to reason, and she wanted to find out where she'd gone wrong in their relationship.

"You don't mind if I stay here for a while, do you?" Kathy stopped beside the car as Trevor got in. "I'll walk to town later or borrow Jed's truck."

"If you need to stay"—Trevor threw a dark look toward the open hangar door where he could see Jed working—"I'll hang around town for an hour or so. Meet me at the post office about two o'clock."

He drove off in a cloud of dust, with Kathy wondering why he should resent her asking to spend a little time with her friends.

Shaking her head at his actions, she wandered slowly to where Jed was lifting the cowling off of a Cessna 152.

"Is that the guy you're working for?" Jed watched the retreating car as it rounded a curve toward town.

"Yes," Kathy admitted. "Funny thing. He really gets uptight in the air. Always makes me fly over the Minam Horse Ranch. You'd think if he was that afraid of flying, he'd drive."

"Not much security in flying over the ranch from where I stand." Jed laid the cowling down and began poking into the engine.

"Have you met the new owner?"

"Of this airplane?" Jed eyed her curiously.

"No, silly, of the Minam Horse Ranch." Kathy pulled up a stool and sat where she could watch him. "Peggy said he visited our house a few times last winter, but I haven't met him yet."

"Nope. Don't even know who he is." Jed seemed lost in thought as he poked and prodded.

"I loved that ranch when Dad and I flew in. I've even thought about applying for the cook's job just for the fun of living there," she rattled on, hoping to get a response. "The stream that runs through the canyon floor is beautiful. And so many interesting people vacation there. Maybe the new owner needs a combination cook, pilot, and bookkeeper." Silence filled the room when she stopped talking.

"Been fishing lately?" Kathy tried another subject, since he didn't seem too interested in the ranch or its new owner.

"Not even once this season." Jed began marking on an order sheet.

"We had some good times." Kathy laughed. "Remember when I snagged my line and you fell in trying to unhook it from that log?"

"As I recall"—Jed walked to the other side of the engine—"you did most of the fishing, and I did most of the work. Never could get you to bait your hook or take the fish off."

"That's what men are for!" Kathy continued laughing at him. "I'd take one look at those great big eyes staring at me and hate myself for hurting them. Only a man is hardhearted enough to handle that."

"I've known a few women who could."

"Well, not me."

They fell silent again while Jed worked. Kathy heard the drone of an airplane as it passed overhead and circled the lake. Jed mumbled something and finally started draining the oil.

"Are you going to be at the parade?" The silence was getting a bit strained. Even that fact puzzled Kathy—since she'd never noticed any strain between them in years past.

"Parade?" Jed seemed to struggle back from far away to talk to her.

"Chief Joseph Days." Kathy's voice held an edge of exasperation. "I just wondered if I'd see you there."

"I doubt it." Jed turned away from her again. "Seems there's always someone in a hurry for me to do something."

"But surely you can take time off for that. No one expects you to work *all* the time."

"Tell you what. *You* go to the parade and the rodeo, and then tell me all about it."

"Sure." Kathy eased off the stool. "Guess I'll go now."

"Yeah. See you." Jed didn't even look up as she left.

Sighing heavily, Kathy walked slowly toward town. It

was more than obvious that she'd been very wrong about her infatuation with Jed.

"It's as though he's a completely different person," she muttered to herself as she strolled past two open fields rapidly filling with horse trailers and campers.

"Hey, watch where you're going!"

A shout caught her attention and she jumped off the road just in time to avoid a truck loaded with horses for the rodeo. The driver shot dark looks at Kathy as he turned in front of her.

Side-jumping the tiny irrigation ditch, Kathy ignored the driver and continued on into town. She turned onto Joseph's Main Street with its Old West storefronts and well-weathered buildings. There were intriguing antique shops, tiny boutiques, and small art galleries shoulder-to-shoulder along the short thoroughfare. The bank and the Manuel Indian and Art Museum were impressive log buildings.

As she sauntered toward the post office, Kathy barely noticed the banners and posters advertising Chief Joseph Days. All around her the town was bursting its seams with a heavy influx of visitors. There was noise and bustle and excitement, but it all seemed to pass her by. Tomorrow was the big parade, but Kathy was so preoccupied she didn't see any of it.

"Going my way? Or were you planning on walking all the way home?"

She looked up just in time to avoid crashing right into Trevor. "Sorry, my thoughts were far away."

"Obviously." Trevor touched her elbow and guided her toward his car. "You walked right in front of a motorhome and didn't even see it!"

"I did?" Kathy turned to see the taillights of a motorhome disappearing around the corner. "Guess I should pay more attention."

"Only if you want to live to the ripe old age of twenty-five!" He opened the car door for her.

Tossing the mail into her lap, he added, "There's a letter from your folks and one from a heartsick boyfriend." He slammed the door and walked around to the other side.

Kathy sorted through the mail and set aside the envelope from her folks. The only other envelope with her name on it was from Lacey.

"You mean *this*?" She held up the envelope with a return address of L. Mills.

"It's your mail," he shrugged, getting into the driver's seat. "You don't owe me any explanation."

"L stands for *Lacey*, my best friend from high school." Kathy ripped open the envelope and unfolded Lacey's mauve stationery.

"Anything important?" Trevor started the car and drove toward the lake.

"If we aren't flying anywhere tomorrow, I'd like to spend the day in town. Lacey's coming for the parade," Kathy explained.

"Right now I don't have any plans," Trevor nodded, "so unless the volcano erupts again or World War III starts, we'll come to town."

"We'll?"

"You don't mind, do you?" He tossed her a rakish smile. "Unless Lacey is a guy and I'd be in the way."

"Lacey is a girl, and you're more than welcome." Actually, Kathy was glad he would be with her. In an odd way she'd come to depend on Trevor—almost as if he were family. In fact, even with Lacey there, the parade wouldn't have been complete without Trevor.

"You'll like her." Kathy smiled. "She's everything I'm not."

"What's that supposed to mean?"

"She doesn't have a temper—and you may have noticed that I do."

"I noticed."

"And she's—"

"If you like her, then I will too. Just relax." Trevor turned into the lane that led to their cabin. "But your temper's not all that bad—most of the time!"

"Thanks. I—"

"She married?"

"No. Why?" Kathy frowned at his quick question.

"Just wondered if there'd be a husband and a passel of kids to contend with."

"Sorry to disappoint you. But as I started to say, she's got great potential as a fashion designer, if she could get the schooling. But right now she and her mother have a dress shop in Pendleton."

That evening Trevor dug out a barbeque from the shed at the back of the camper. Lighting the coals, he insisted that he would cook dinner. A holiday air lightened the mood, and Kathy relaxed. There had been so much tension and formality between them that this was a very welcome change.

"This is dinner?" Kathy wrinkled her nose playfully when Trevor proudly served barbequed hot dogs and baked beans.

"Corn on the cob, coming up." Trevor strode to his camper and returned with two steaming ears still wrapped in their husks.

"Beggars can't be choosers," Kathy shrugged, filling her plate.

"I've been mighty grateful for all the cooking you've done this summer." Trevor cocked an eyebrow in her direction. "But once in a while we ought to eat like everyone else in the park."

It was all so intimate, just the two of them sitting on the patio like old married folks, licking their fingers and bantering playfully. "Want some chocolate cake?" Kathy offered. "I made one yesterday, just in case."

"In case?" Trevor looked up, surprised.

"That's Mom's favorite excuse for baking." Kathy gathered up the dirty dishes. "In case company comes, in case someone has a chocolate attack, in case it rains. . . ."

"In that case—yes!"

She produced the cake, sliced off two thick chunks topped with a fudge frosting, and proudly placed one plate in front of Trevor.

"Didn't anyone in your family ever bake just for the fun of it?" Kathy had never asked about his family, but she surmised if they were living, they didn't live nearby.

"Gram did. Oh, the cookies she pulled from the oven!" Trevor smacked his lips.

Although Kathy assumed he wasn't married, he'd never said whether he'd ever been married, divorced, widowed, or even had a serious girlfriend. Of course there was Cynthia, but he never talked about her either. In fact, Kathy hadn't been able to get him to talk about his background at all. Maybe this was the time.

"Not your mother . . . or your wife?" She kept her eyes riveted on her plate, afraid of his response.

"My mother could cook when she wanted to." He toyed with his fork. "But most of the time she preferred to concentrate on her work and let someone else do the cooking."

Silence stretched tautly while Kathy waited.

When she'd held her breath to the snapping point, she prompted, "And your . . . wife?"

Clearing his throat roughly, Trevor shrugged, "Let's just leave it at that, shall we? And since I slaved over the hot coals to provide *your* dinner, I'd love to watch you do the dishes."

The twinkle in his eyes eased the tension, but Kathy avoided looking directly at him while she cleared the table; she was embarrassed at her question.

In the morning Kathy tucked a green-and-blue plaid western shirt into slender jeans. The fringe on the dipped back yoke swished softly as she moved around the house.

"Nice." Trevor commented on her outfit when she stepped outside. "You ought to wear western clothes more often."

"You look like you were born in them," Kathy returned the compliment. "Do you always wear clothes that match your eyes?" His blue-checkered shirt tapered neatly over his lean body, fitting snugly into well-worn jeans. There was just a touch of western embroidery on the front and back yoke of his shirt.

"I didn't know you even knew what color my eyes were," he grinned, gallantly tipping his snappy cowboy hat.

Their mood was obviously light and filled with holiday anticipation as they drove toward town along the narrow road around the lake. Beneath a fringe of eyelashes, Kathy covertly studied his face.

If he ever was married, she thought, *his wife must have enjoyed his looks.*

"Penny for your thoughts," Trevor abruptly turned, catching her gaze.

"I, uh, was just thinking"—she struggled quickly for something to say—"what a nice hat you have! I probably should get one."

"That'll be the first thing on our agenda." Trevor maneuvered the car into a parking place near the laundromat.

"I'm going to find Lacey first." Kathy climbed out of the car.

"Oh yes, I forgot." Trevor teased, locking the car. "Mustn't buy anything without the fashion expert." Then, tucking her arm through his, he pulled her tightly against him to avoid the jostling crowd. Their sudden touch was like an electric jolt. It forcefully reminded her of the unusual effect he had on her when they were this close.

It unnerved her so much she pulled away from him suddenly. "I . . . I think I'll search for Lacey." She shoved her hands into her pockets. "She should be here by now. Is there someplace we can meet?"

Frowning, Trevor eyed her slowly. "Whatever you want. I'll be near the museum when you're ready."

Unable to meet his questioning eyes, Kathy just nodded and escaped as quickly as possible. "There's something about that man . . ." she muttered, virtually racing away from him.

"Man? What man? Where?" Lacey's voice penetrated her thoughts.

"Oh, you scared me to death," Kathy gasped, looking up to see her friend leaning on the wooden rail in front of the restaurant.

"I want to know—what man? Where?" Lacey grinned. "If you're so deep in thought about him, I want to meet him."

"Oh, it's nothing important. Just Trevor." Kathy stepped up on the boardwalk beside her. "We're supposed to meet him by the museum."

"I'm dying to meet this . . . mystery man. Isn't that what you called him in your first letter to me?" Lacey was obviously enjoying Kathy's agitation.

"Oh, Lacey, you wouldn't tell him?"

"Only if I thought it was important," Lacey teased. "Come on. Lead me to him."

The girls shouldered their way toward the museum, dodging kids with enormous bags of sticky cotton candy. Everywhere people were uniformly dressed in western gear. Jeans, cowboy boots, hats, embroidered shirts of plain, plaid, or checkered designs decked bodies of every size.

Half a block off Main Street the shrieks of kids on a roller coaster mingled with the ever-present carnival music.

Stalls and booths lined the streets where vendors hawked their colorful wares.

"There he is," Kathy spotted Trevor just ahead.

"Which one?" Lacey swept the crowd with her eyes.

"The tall dark-haired man. See the blue-checkered shirt?"

"You don't mean that gorgeous hunk is your boss?" Lacey turned to stare at Kathy. "You never told me what he looked like. I'd have been here sooner—much sooner!"

"That didn't take long." Trevor strode toward them. "I presume this is Lacey?" He reached out a strong hand to shake hers, obviously sweeping her turquoise-clad form from head to toe. "I didn't realize Kathy had such good taste in friends."

"Trevor, this is Lacey." Kathy tried to ignore a strange lump in her throat as Trevor held Lacey's hand. "Lacey, this is—"

"Trevor." Lacey dipped her knees in a mock curtsey. "And I didn't realize Kathy had such a gallant employer."

Kathy frowned at her own agitation as she watched their eyes lock in some strange message. It was as though they already knew each other. Or worse, were instantly attracted to each other.

First Cynthia and now Lacey. What is this? Jealousy? Trying to deny the unusual emotion, Kathy clenched her teeth. *Can't be. I'm just imagining things.*

"So you're interested in fashion," Trevor was saying when Kathy tuned in to their voices again. "Now I can see why. That's a great outfit."

"Thank you," Lacey bubbled. "Mom and I try to keep a few secrets. One of them is that I often design and make my own clothes. It wouldn't do for the customers to think I don't wear our own merchandise."

"Your secret's safe with me," Trevor reached for both women, pulling them to either side of him. Placing an arm around each of their shoulders, he walked proudly between them.

"I think you've come just in time." Trevor bent his head toward Lacey. "I promised Kathy I'd buy her a cowboy hat, but we need your expertise."

"Just like old times, right?" Lacey leaned in front of him to smile at Kathy. "I've been helping Kathy pick out clothes as long as I can remember."

"Couldn't have survived without you," Kathy mumbled, trying to return her friend's smile. *What's the matter with me? Maybe it's not me, maybe it's them,* she reasoned. *They're treating me like I'm not here—or like I'm a helpless two-year-old.*

Satisfied that she'd identified the source of her irritation, Kathy forced a smile to her lips and tried to ignore the animosity she felt.

Stopping in front of a booth piled high with cowboy hats, Trevor grabbed a bright green one and plunked it on her head. "How's that?" he laughed as her eyes disappeared beneath the enormous brim.

"It's a bit much, don't you think?" Kathy lifted the obviously too large hat and handed it back to the clerk.

"How about this one," Lacey reached for a delicate blue hat trimmed with a hatband of soft blue and green feathers. "Look at the way it brings out the color of her eyes."

Kathy admired the hat in the mirror tacked to one post of the booth. She had to admit Lacey knew her stuff.

Tucking one strand of blond hair behind her ear, she said, "I love it. Once again I bow to the exquisite taste of Lacey Mills." Kathy hugged her friend, sorry she'd harbored even a shade of jealousy toward her. "What do you think, Trevor?"

When she looked up to seek his answer, their eyes locked and he seemed to hold his breath.

"I think . . . ." he let out a strangely ragged sound, "you're absolutely beautiful in that hat." He raised one hand and tilted the hat jauntily to one side. "We'll take it."

Turning around, Kathy noticed the crowds lining Main Street, apparently waiting for the parade. "Looks as if it's time for the main attraction. Shall we go?"

Lacey nodded and started toward the street with Kathy close behind her. Trevor insisted on paying for the hat himself, then joined them just as they found a vantage point on the museum steps.

"Thanks." Kathy suddenly felt shy as she watched Trevor take three giant steps to stand beside her. "The hat is lovely."

"Lovely gift for a lovely lady." Trevor grinned, leaning back against the building.

10

The Chief Joseph Days parade started with a loud bang. Moments later the crowd clapped as the parade marshall rode into view on an antique fire truck.

Behind him marched the first of several high-school bands from the surrounding area. Next, on a well-groomed Palomino, the Queen of the Umatilla County Fair rode by fully garbed in beaded and feathered regalia.

Overhead, three antique airplanes made several passes crisscrossing Main Street, the last pass ending with a slow roll.

The master of ceremonies, perched in a yellow van with loudspeakers on all four corners, bantered with each group as it passed, bringing laughs from the clowns and blushes to the cheeks of the young women.

There were horses, horses, and more horses. No western parade was complete without all the local riding clubs getting into the act. Each group paused by the announcer to execute their special drill.

"Enjoying yourself, Trevor?" Kathy asked and raised an eyebrow in a smirk when she saw him openly admiring a slender feminine rider with waist-length blond hair.

"Any reason I shouldn't?" He grinned at her, then turned to Lacey. "Will you be coming out to the cabin with us after the parade is over?"

"I—" Lacey glanced at Kathy with a tiny frown. "I don't think so, but thank you for asking." She quickly returned her attention to the parade.

"I'd planned on staying in town with Lacey," Kathy said to Trevor. "Is there any reason we have to go back right away?" A noisy entry in the parade drowned out his answer with loud explosions from their muskets. Oddly dressed mountain men scrambled off an ancient truck that was belching smoke.

"What?" Kathy prompted when the noise had passed.

"No reason. Let's just enjoy." Trevor's answer was maddening. He seemed to include himself in everything they did.

Because the street was so short, the parade made a second pass. Then the crowd surged out to enjoy the booths again. Kathy and Lacey sauntered across the street to a jewelry stand.

"I love this stuff," Lacey touched a turquoise pendant set in handcrafted silver.

"It would just match your outfit," Trevor's voice, directly behind her, startled Kathy.

"I thought we lost you." Kathy made a face at him.

"No such luck." Trevor placed a hand on her shoulder, sending warm tingles radiating up her neck. "With two lovely women to escort, no red-blooded American male would pass up this chance."

"I don't mind." Lacey flashed a delicate smile at him and glanced toward Kathy, obviously tossing the ball to her.

"Uh, sure. We'd be glad to have you tag along," she reluctantly agreed. There seemed to be something going on beneath the surface between Lacey and Trevor, and for some reason she couldn't explain, Kathy didn't like it.

I'll have to talk to her later, Kathy decided. *She doesn't want to get involved with a man like him. He's just not her type.*

The day was an odd mixture of fun and strain for Kathy. The three of them were never separated. Kathy puzzled over Trevor's attitude. He treated both girls equally, yet she often caught him locked in eye contact with Lacey when they thought she wasn't looking.

It was almost a relief when Lacey finally admitted she needed to leave. "The drive back to Pendleton is going to be long, and I don't like driving through the mountains after dark."

"I'd have Kathy fly you home," Trevor countered, "but I know you brought your car. Be sure and come again, if you can. Kathy and I would really enjoy it."

"I probably won't be able to get away again this summer." Lacey ducked her head as she climbed into her car. "But thanks anyway. See you, Kathy," she waved.

As they turned away from her departing car, Trevor placed his arm lightly across Kathy's shoulders, guiding her toward their car.

"I've seen about all of this I want to see. If it's okay with you"—he cocked his head to look at her—"I'd really like to go back home."

"Sure," Kathy agreed, wondering if the celebration had lost its flavor for him because Lacey was gone.

"She's a nice girl." Trevor glanced over his shoulder one more time in the direction Lacey had gone. "I'm glad she came. Except for the week of your cousin's wedding, you've been pretty isolated from your family and friends."

They drove silently around the lake and back to the cabin, the day coming to a dissatisfying close.

———

Ten more days passed uneventfully, and Kathy was beginning to acquire a good tan from spending so much time on the beach. As usual, the campgrounds were filled to capacity. There was an air of lazy anticipation as she strolled between tents and trailers. Smoke from the campfires swirled around her, pungent with roasting hot dogs.

One shimmering afternoon Kathy and Trevor rented a foot-operated paddleboat. Treading the tiny two-person version of a stern-wheeler, they broke free of the shore and slowly churned through the smooth water. Far out on the lake, water-skiers zigzagged in the sparkling spray while die-hard fishermen trolled the green depths.

The sun burned warmly on Kathy's skin and sent trickles of salty sweat running down her face and arms. When the heat became too intense, Trevor stopped paddling and they slid off into the cool water.

Kathy rolled over on her back and floated, watching fleecy clouds drift across the sky. Rolling onto her stomach, she spied Trevor swimming in a wide lazy circle around her and the paddleboat. *Trevor has become so important to me, yet I know so little about him. He just seems to dominate my life right now.*

Then, pushing away from that train of thought because it made her uneasy, she slipped into a prayer. *I still need your guidance for my life. Open the right doors for me, God. The summer will soon be gone, and Trevor will go away—and I still don't know what I should be doing.*

She gasped as a strong yank on her ankles pulled her under water. Immediately, she was shoved upward, and sunlight flooded her dripping face.

"Gotcha!" Trevor surfaced beside her and laughed as she sputtered. A strong, tanned arm lightly encircled her shoulders while she caught her breath.

"Ogre!" Kathy playfully shoved against him, splashing water in his face.

"Think the Wallowa Lake monster got you?" Trevor teased. "Those toes would look mighty tempting if he'd seen them before I did!"

"The only monster here is you," she countered, surprised by his sudden playfulness. The sun sparkled on the water drops on his face, but it was the sparkle in his eyes that snared her attention. She couldn't seem to look away.

They bobbed silently, inches apart in the water, neither

one speaking, neither one breaking eye contact. The moment lasted forever.

Suddenly a motor roared past them, destroying the mood as waves from a speedboat broke over them. Kathy twisted and stroked toward their paddleboat. When she reached it, she grabbed the edge of the seat and pulled herself back into place. Trevor silently joined her on the hot seat and aimed the boat toward land.

Children splashed in the roped-off swimming area as Kathy and Trevor came back into shore. It had been a glorious afternoon.

———

"Vacations are such a special time," Kathy mused aloud that evening. She sat alone on her porch and watched the families in the trailer park gather around their campfires, remembering times when her own family had gone camping. She stood up and stretched.

"All this rest is getting to me," she muttered into the shadows. "If things don't perk up around here, I think I'll ask Mr. Trevor Kingston if I can go home."

"Did I hear you take my name in vain?"

Kathy dropped her arms and whirled around to face him. As much as she'd been around Trevor, she still reacted strongly every time he came near. She'd given up trying to analyze why.

Bracing herself, she watched him get up lazily from the step of the camper where he obviously had been sitting for some time.

"How long have you been there?" Kathy wondered just how much he had heard.

"Long enough to know you're getting bored." He stepped lightly down and approached her, one hand tucked into his pocket.

"Well, it's true." She waited to see his reaction. "If you

don't need me, I'd like to fly home to see my family."

"Actually I do need you." Trevor stepped up beside her, sending the anticipated tingles up her spine. "But not as a pilot. In all that fancy schooling you got, did you happen to learn how to type?"

"Mom insisted on it," Kathy answered, thinking he was much too close. She couldn't step backward, or she'd fall off the porch.

"Good for your mom." Trevor absently reached up and brushed the hair back from her face; it was warm where his fingers had touched her skin. "I've been working on some reports and could really use some help—if you don't mind?"

"Why not?" Kathy shrugged and smiled. Anything would be better than just sitting around.

"Good." He slipped his arm around her waist to help her down the steps. "I've got it all set up, but it's kind of crowded in that camper. Maybe we could move it to the kitchen table?" He nodded toward her cabin.

————

Hours later she gratefully accepted a cup of coffee and rubbed her stiffened fingers. He had to have been joking when he claimed it was "all set up." It had taken nearly two hours to straighten out the pages of figures. Even with her business degree, the numbers didn't mean much to her. It had taken several more hours to type column after column of exacting numbers. They appeared to be a budget for a hotel or resort, but since he offered no explanation, she didn't ask for one.

"Two more pages and I'll be finished." Kathy wrapped her fingers around the warm cup. "Believe me, Trevor. You need a secretary!"

"I know," he laughed, "but until I get one, you'll do just fine." He leaned across the back of her chair, and Kathy could feel the warmth of his breath on her neck.

"It would have taken me a month to type all this with my fastest two-finger approach." He straightened up, and Kathy felt something brush the top of her hair.

Probably just his sleeve, she thought, leaning toward the typewriter again. Yet in the back of her mind, she couldn't escape the feeling that he'd kissed her hair.

When she'd finished, they sat in the gentle night hours on the porch. Silently he massaged her taut neck and shoulder muscles, probing with deep circles to relax her tension. When she turned to thank him, he bent his head and brushed her lips lightly with his. It was so swift and gentle she almost wasn't sure it had happened, but her senses confirmed it in neon signals.

"Thanks," he murmured in her ear, "I really appreciate all your help." Then he strode swiftly off the porch toward his camper, exposing in Kathy an aching void that she had not known existed. It took a long time for her to fall asleep that night, and when she did, her dreams were filled with Trevor's blue eyes and dimpled smile. Tender lips repeatedly taunted and touched her own. As daylight crept beneath the drapes she finally slept peacefully. She woke to a full sun.

It was just a thank-you kiss, she thought for the hundredth time. Still mulling over the night before, she wandered toward the kitchen. A note propped beside the coffee on the stove caught her attention.

GONE FISHING was printed in big block letters at the top. Beneath it in clear, round handwriting Trevor had written: *Thought you deserved a break today. So sleep late, relax, have a cup of coffee, and I'll be back about noon.* His initialed R.A.K. seemed incongruously formal compared to the note.

Kathy smiled, filling her empty cup from the percolator that he'd left piping hot. "Thanks for the coffee, Sir

Trevor." She raised her cup in absent salute, then stopped. "Must still have him up on that white horse."

She frowned and took her cup into the living room. "This has got to stop," she scolded herself. "You hardly know the man—and look at you. You're on as much of a romantic roller coaster as Peggy!"

Suddenly she sat down and pressed her fingers against her hot cheeks as the truth penetrated. Romantic! Was it possible that she was falling in love with him? But she hardly knew him.

"No!" She jumped up and started pacing the room. "It can't be. I've only just met him, and he's much older than I am. And . . . and there's Cynthia too . . . and Jed . . ." But no matter how much she protested, the idea just wouldn't go away. A car pulled up outside, and Kathy determined that Trevor would never know what she'd just been thinking. After all, he'd never indicated any special feelings for her. In fact, most of the time it seemed just the opposite.

"Besides," she reasoned, "maybe it's a temporary crush." Casually she sauntered out onto the porch with her steaming cup of coffee.

"Good morning, or should I say afternoon?" Trevor smiled broadly, dumping his fishing gear onto the ground. "Did you sleep well?"

"Hello yourself. I slept very well. And thank you for the coffee." Kathy answered, waving the cup in his direction. She stayed firmly on the porch. "How was fishing?" *That will be a safe subject,* she thought.

"Caught some nice little Kokanee." He lifted his creel, and the pungent odor of fish permeated the air.

"Down by the dam?" she asked, remembering that Jed used to take her fishing there. At his surprised nod, she decided to impress him with her knowledge. "I love that pink meat. Most people don't realize that Wallowa Lake has a species of landlocked salmon. They're delicious fried, or even grilled."

"I didn't realize you were such a fisherwoman." Trevor sat down on the steps to remove his boots. A lock of dark brown hair fell across his eyes. "Maybe you should have gone with me this morning instead of lazing in bed."

"I enjoyed my sleep, but thanks anyway."

"Want to take a picnic lunch to the top of the mountain?"

"That sounds good," she answered, weighing in a split second her newly named emotions for him against a panic that said she should stay as far away from him as possible. Instantly capitulating, she added, "But I suppose you expect *me* to provide the lunch?"

"Naturally." He grinned, jumping up and going into his trailer before she could answer.

"Glad to oblige," she retorted softly, knowing he couldn't hear. "Maybe a little arsenic in your Thermos will change your opinion!"

She started opening cupboard doors and soon was busy fixing ham and cheese sandwiches on thick slices of whole wheat bread. While some eggs boiled, she finally located a basket in the storage room and filled it to capacity with their lunch.

"That's a definite improvement," she said approvingly as Trevor came through her open door and into the kitchen. She sniffed his woodsy cologne. "Fish never was my favorite fragrance!"

Clad in blue jeans with a matching blue plaid cotton shirt, his sleeves were rolled back, revealing tanned, muscular arms. Kathy caught her breath as his personality seemed to fill the room.

She turned quickly back to examine their lunch. *No sense in letting him see what a silly crush I have on him,* she thought.

But crushes were for teenagers like Peggy—and Kathy knew this was more than a crush.

"You're not bad-looking today either." Trevor gave her a dimpled grin. "But you ought to change shoes," he suggested. "Open sandals might not be too comfortable for walking up there." He jerked a thumb toward the mountain.

It only took a moment to change into her sturdy flight shoes. "These ought to work," she raised a tiny foot for him to see. "Anything beats getting dirt and rocks under my toes."

"You're improving," he nodded, picking up the basket she'd provided and opening the screen door. "I fully expected an argument."

She laughed at the truth of what he said. "My dad always said I'd argue with Saint Peter about the color of heaven's gates. But"—she stepped through the door he held open for her—"when it comes to important things, I'll yield to the truth anytime."

11

*T*he sun shone warmly, filtering through the trees as they walked along the dirt road. Kathy, her pulse racing at Trevor's nearness, decided to relax and enjoy being with him. There were so many unanswered questions.

How involved was he with Cynthia? What about the way he acted around Lacey? And he still had never been straightforward about his marital status. Kathy pushed the nagging thoughts aside. He didn't seem like the type to lead a woman on.

They stopped on the old log bridge and watched the water rush and tumble over the rocks. Then, as their dusty lane approached the pavement, two deer bounded across the fence in front of them, followed quickly by a third.

The afternoon air was filled with the happy sounds of kids riding go-carts. Returning hikers called to one another, and mothers reminded little ones to be careful around the traffic.

Just as they reached the gondola, Kathy spotted the Swiss-styled souvenir boutique. "Could we go in? They have such cute things. . . ." Her question trailed off into a smile when she caught Trevor's look of indulgence.

"Never knew a woman who could resist shopping," he shrugged, yielding to her plea. "Especially at the only store in the park."

Inside, one section of the store was devoted to Alpine hiking and skiing gear. A heavy rack of boots filled the open area in front of a brick fireplace. There were unusual pieces of pottery, jewelry, and even a selection of Swiss candy. Kathy paused at a display of cups. She chose one with a cute bear to take to Peggy, but Trevor stopped her.

"One bear is enough," he reminded her of the large stuffed one that waited in her bedroom. "Let's get something today that focuses on you, not your sister." He glanced along the shelf and reached for another cup.

"Now this one is definitely you!" He held up the cup with a delicate pastel horse and butterfly.

"A horse?" Kathy was puzzled. "Why?"

"It's beautiful." He touched her chin with the tip of his finger. "And graceful—but most of all," he firmly steered her toward the cash register, "it's the key to a wonderful promise."

Kathy was shocked at his gentleness. It seemed out of character when she compared it to the brisk businessman she'd seen so often. But then, there'd been changes in both of them since last night that were difficult to explain.

"I didn't know you were so poetic," she teased him, tucking the cup carefully into their picnic basket once they were outside.

"There's a lot you don't know about me." He spoke almost harshly. Then, taking her hand in an automatic gesture, he guided her across the road. "Come on. Let's catch the gondola. It's a long ride to the top, and I'm hungry."

They crunched up the gravel path to a large old-board building and climbed into a two-man glass-enclosed gondola. When Kathy sat facing Trevor, her back was toward the view.

"Sit over here." Trevor moved to one side of the small seat.

She shook her head, not wanting to test herself by sitting that close to him.

"The view is better from here." He pulled her toward

him just as the gondola started with a jerk, and she landed in a pile against his chest. For a moment, neither of them moved. The ground gave way beneath them, leaving Kathy a bit dizzy. She knew it wasn't from the swaying of their car.

Together they extricated themselves from the tangle. When she was finally seated—or stuffed—beside him, it was another moment before he spoke.

"Next time," he said, his voice deep and husky, "just trust me."

The world around them swiftly changed as they rose up the face of the mountain. Treetops whispered just beneath their cubicle as they dipped and swayed on the cable high over the ground. Below them the lake appeared as a turquoise jewel on the edge of a green velvet gown.

As they climbed higher, the arid moraine and flatland beyond it showed a dusty brown. Kathy closed her eyes briefly, sensing a strange tingling that spread throughout her body. Her breath came in short snatches.

Nearing the top of the cable ride, the lake became small and insignificant. It appeared as only a drop of water edged in a flat, tan haze.

A stiff breeze swayed their car, and Kathy unconsciously put a hand against Trevor's arm to steady herself. She felt him shift into the corner and put his arm around her shoulders. His touch sent her heart beating so rapidly, Kathy wondered if he could hear it.

The ride seemed to take forever, but it wasn't nearly long enough. When they opened the door and entered the terminal at the top, Kathy suddenly realized they hadn't spoken during the ride.

Just being near him, she thought, *I'll remember that ride for the rest of my life.*

"Let's buy some peanuts." Trevor, too, seemed to shake himself free of the moment. "We'll feed the ground squirrels later."

Kathy turned into the wind as it blew her hair back from her face. She took the sack of peanuts Trevor bought and fell into step beside him. He shifted the picnic basket to the opposite hand and started down the path.

"I hope you don't mind a little hike before we eat." He cleared his throat. "There's a nice spot with a terrific view out on this point, away from the crowds."

Kathy just nodded, still not trusting herself to talk. The ride had shaken her more deeply than she cared to admit. It was going to be difficult not letting him see her love.

And it is love, she finally admitted. She was ready to accept the consequences, knowing he would never love her in return.

At last they chose a place with some flat rocks, and Kathy unpacked their food. She placed plastic cups on a small cloth while Trevor reached for the tall Thermos.

He filled one cup, but rummaged in the basket until he found the horse cup. Wiping it first with a napkin, he filled it with coffee and handed it to her.

"Here, drink this. You'll feel better." When she looked at him quizzically, he added, "You looked a bit peaked on the ride up here. I have to admit I was surprised. Most people who can fly an airplane don't have problems with the gondola."

"Thanks." She accepted the cup and drank deeply. It was easier just to let him think she'd been motion sick rather than to tell him the truth. At least she knew now why he had put his arm around her in the gondola.

"Now that you've drunk from it and the cup is really yours," he said, "I want you to know I bought it for another reason." He paused and stared into the distance. "I can't tell you why—at least not right now. Just remember"—his eyes sought hers, drawing her into their depths—"if anything ever happens, there's a hidden message in the cup."

"You sound so mysterious." Kathy reluctantly broke eye

contact. "What message could possibly be hidden in a horse and a butterfly?" She twisted the cup, trying to decipher his message.

Failing to unravel his puzzle, she added, "And what do you mean 'if anything happens'? I don't understand." She suddenly put the cup down, nearly spilling the coffee.

"I can't explain right now, Kathy." He searched her face intently, almost tenderly. "Maybe I shouldn't have said even this much." He sighed audibly. "Just forget it, okay?" He picked up a sandwich and selected one of the boiled eggs Kathy was peeling.

When they'd finished, Kathy pulled an apple out of the basket, cut it in two, and handed him half. "There was only one left in the refrigerator. It's all I could find for dessert."

Trevor munched on its crispness while they gathered up the lunch remains.

Kathy's hands shook when she touched him accidentally as they piled things in the basket. *This is silly,* she scolded herself. *If you're not careful, he'll know something is wrong!*

Feeding the ground squirrels a little later on another section of the trail, Kathy sat on a rock and drank in the beauty of the Wallowa Mountains. Their grandeur seemed so out of place when contrasted with the flat land leading up to them. The valleys dropped dizzily in several directions.

"Kathy," Trevor interrupted her quiet study of the horizon.

"What?" She turned, a nut in her open palm.

"Oh . . . nothing." Trevor changed his mind as a group of sightseers surged over the hill. "We'll talk about it later."

"Oh, look!" A little boy squealed, pointing toward Kathy's feet.

She looked down and saw a rather bold little squirrel resting against her shoe as it tried desperately to reach the food in her hand. Gently Kathy lowered her hand, and the squirrel gratefully scooped up the nut and scampered across the rocks.

"Ready?" Trevor stood and shook out the empty sack. He reached for her hand to help her up, not letting go as they started down the path.

"These trees are so unusual," she commented as they passed a patch on the left. "They're so dwarfed and twisted by the wind that they really look more like grotesque bushes than trees."

"The wind can do amazing things," Trevor agreed. "It can change a tree . . . change a life."

Kathy looked up quickly at the strange tone in his voice, but his face was inscrutable. "Change a life?"

"Never mind. I guess I'm in an odd mood." He drew her hand up into the crook of his arm as they stepped off the path to allow some children to pass.

Feeling his muscles flex and relax beneath her hand gave Kathy a flutter in the pit of her stomach. She knew he meant nothing personal. He'd have tucked his grandmother's hand in his arm in exactly the same way.

When they were almost back to the gondola terminal, Trevor stopped and pointed into the distance. "You can see the airport from here. It's in that open space just beyond the town."

She nodded, not wanting to remind him that she'd been here many times. In fact, the airport looked much like this when she made an approach over the lake.

"Well, we can't put it off much longer." Trevor picked up the depleted picnic basket and started toward the gondola. "We have to go down the mountain sometime. This is the only way. Think you're ready to handle it?"

"Certainly," Kathy answered with more bravado than she felt. It wasn't the swaying car that she was worried about; it was being so close to him.

But she needn't have worried. Although he sat beside

her, this time Trevor spent the whole time talking. He was trying to divert her attention by pointing out interesting scenes on the mountain facing them. She let him talk, welcoming any distraction from his physical nearness.

As they reached her cabin door, Trevor opened it with one hand, placing the picnic basket on the steps. His other arm curved around her, gently touching her back. He turned to look at her. There was a look of contentment on his face. Kathy felt a flicker of hope run through her breast. The timing was perfect, if . . .

"Trevie, I'm so glad you're back," Cynthia's voice sliced the air between them, causing Trevor to mutter under his breath. His face altered to the more familiar business lines. "I've been waiting for hours," she trilled.

Cynthia stepped out onto the porch. "Oh . . . Miss Evans. What are *you* doing here?" Then her eyes widened, and she said sweetly, "Are those *your* things in Mother's room?" She backed into the cabin as Kathy and Trevor followed. "Trevie, couldn't you find a room for her at the lodge?"

"I didn't try." Trevor retrieved the basket and handed it to Kathy. "Put this away, will you?"

His tone and piercing look were so pointed, Kathy obeyed without saying a word. *So this cabin belongs to Cynthia,* she thought. *No wonder he hesitated when he said it belonged to a friend. And stupid me*—she shoved the basket harshly onto a shelf—*in about thirty more seconds I'd have fallen into his well-planned trap.* She picked up the horse cup and washed it along with the other dishes.

Angry at the sudden stinging in her eyes, Kathy blinked furiously and nearly slammed the cup onto the counter. *And I thought the cup was something special. No wonder he sounded so poetic.* She burned at the memory. *Beautiful. Graceful. And it holds such promise,* she mocked his words. *He's had enough practice to cause a statue to swoon. Well, this statue just turned to ice!*

She put the rest of the dishes away, and then as an afterthought picked up the cup to check it. Satisfied that it was still in one piece, she left the cup in plain sight on the counter.

As Kathy made her way back into the living room, Cynthia moved quickly one step back from Trevor, her black hair still nearly touching his shoulder.

"Anyway, I'd still be waiting," Cynthia went on, barely glancing in Kathy's direction, "except some nice young man offered to drive me out here. Maybe *you* know him," she turned and included Kathy. "He has curly red hair and the cutest green eyes and lots of freckles—his name is Jud something."

"Jed," Kathy corrected. "Jed James. He works at the airport."

"I was sure you'd know him," Cynthia smiled, satisfied. "Somehow with all that grease, I just knew he'd be one of your friends."

Kathy opened her mouth to retort, then closed her lips firmly. No sense playing right into the spider's web.

"Actually, in spite of the grease," Kathy said as she edged toward the hall, "Jed's quite nice once you get to know him. In fact, we're *very* close friends."

Trevor's head snapped up, and his eyes narrowed dangerously. There was a hard look she'd never noticed before.

"That's odd." Cynthia, too, seemed to stiffen. "Jed didn't mention he had a girlfriend when I asked him to come back for a barbeque tonight. You'll have to watch him . . . I think he has a wandering eye." Cynthia raised a knowing eyebrow at Kathy and meaningfully smoothed her red silk lounging outfit.

Turning on her heel, Kathy controlled every step, consciously suppressing the urge to run. Not until she was safely behind the closed bedroom door did she realize she'd been holding her breath. She hadn't meant Jed and she were *that* close, but Cynthia made her so confused she hadn't thought to deny it.

"Now why did I say that?" she flung at her image in the mirror. "I only meant to silence her. Jed will disown me if he finds out." She thought of him coming to the barbeque. "What next?" She spread her hands in frustration.

"That's what I'd like to know!"

She whirled in time to see Trevor close the door behind him. His face like a thundercloud, he stood firmly in place, barricading her escape. "Why didn't you tell me about your *relationship* with Jed?" His arms akimbo, hands clamped on his hips, he looked like a football middle-linebacker guarding the goal.

"You didn't ask." She stalled for time, trying to decide how best to set him straight. Being alone with him in this bedroom was overpowering. Only by forcing herself to re-call that Cynthia was outside and that Trevor was playing games with whichever woman was available was she able to stand firm. "Besides, you sort of neglected to tell me about your relationship with Cynthia," she countered, "so I don't see what you're all upset about."

"What do you mean?" He covered the distance between them in two long strides.

"Jed's here," Cynthia called through the closed door. "Will you start the fire, or shall I?"

"Go ahead," he snapped. "I'll be there in a minute."

When they heard her move away from the door, Kathy lifted an eyebrow and said, "I think your 'fire' is waiting."

He stepped aside, nodding toward the door. "I think you'd better go too. Your *friend* is here."

He opened the door, and Kathy escaped into the hall-way, but not before she detected a slight, but puzzling, droop to his shoulders. The joy of her afternoon on the mountain with Trevor was gone. There was no hope that he'd ever return her love. In fact, he had suddenly become a different person.

An aching need ripped through her heart as she realized that she needed help beyond any human assistance to end this chaos. *Help me, Lord,* she prayed quickly, agony burning in her heart. *I can't handle this alone.*

Kathy felt thoroughly confused as she hurried outside. Somehow she had to get Jed alone and talk to him—fast!

12

$\mathscr{I}$t was too late. When she opened the door, there stood Cynthia looking dainty and helpless while Jed prepared the barbeque fire. Kathy wet her lips and tried to think of something to say.

"Hello, *sweetheart*." Jed looked up, his eyes raking her from head to toe in a look she'd never experienced before. "Come and help me with the fire."

Kathy edged toward him, wondering how she could talk to him alone. This wasn't going to be easy. If only she'd thought before making that crazy outburst!

"Jed, I . . . I'm glad Cynthia asked you to join us," she hedged. "We just haven't had much time together this summer, have we?" There really wasn't anything she could do to help with the fire. Jed had already finished.

"That's what I told Cynthia when she pouted because we hadn't told her of our . . . relationship." He put out an arm and drew Kathy close, squeezing her tightly at his side as her fears were confirmed. "But we'll make up for it beginning right now."

He cocked his head toward Cynthia. "You'll excuse us for a few minutes, won't you? That fire is all set, and it'll be a while before the coals are ready. Maybe Kathy and I can slip away for a walk."

"Go right ahead." Cynthia gave them a smirk. "Trevie and I have some catching up to do, too. Just take your time." She turned gracefully, red silk swinging in motion with her black hair, and went back into the cabin leaving them alone.

"Jed, I'm sorry," Kathy spoke quickly when they were alone. "But thanks for backing me up. I don't know what made me tell them we're such . . . close friends."

"Never mind that," he pulled her away from the cabin. "We need to talk. Besides, it might work out best this way." He grasped her hand tightly and turned onto a path leading into the trees.

"Honest, I was just joking . . . and sort of desperate." Kathy ran to keep up with him and tripped on a protruding root. She fell hard and bit back a cry of pain.

Jed stopped and pulled her up. "Are you okay?"

"Yes, just dirty I guess." She brushed off her shorts and wondered if the stain would come out. "Where are we going in such a hurry?"

"This is far enough, I guess." Jed sat on the stump of a dead pine, his face engulfed in the shadows of twilight.

With no room beside him on the stump, Kathy sought the support of a living fir. Padding the ground near its roots with a handful of green leaves from a nearby bush, she leaned against its towering strength.

"Kathy," he appeared to hesitate, then plunged ahead. "We can talk about our personal relationship later. It might not be such a bad idea. You're good-looking enough, and I've always liked you. But right now I need a favor—a big one—and as my girlfriend, it'll be that much easier for you."

Jed had changed from his usual jeans into a gray T-shirt and black denims. In the shadows, all Kathy could see was his face.

"You remember Frank?" he asked briskly.

"How could I forget? That whole thing in Spokane seemed almost sinister."

"You're catching on." Jed shifted on the stump as he uncrossed his legs. "I need to get another package to him—quickly."

"I can't," Kathy shuddered as she thought of Frank and the darkness in Spokane. "I'm hired out to Trevor, and I don't know where or when he'll want to fly."

"Get him to go somewhere—anywhere in the Spokane area will do."

"Why can't you put it on the bus?" Kathy shifted her feet, seeking the last rays of the sun. "What's so important about all this?"

"Don't ask so many questions." Jed's voice was harsh. "Just do as you're told. Promise Trevor anything, but get him to go."

"You mean lie? I'm already in enough trouble for exaggerating about you and me." Kathy shook her head. "And I'm going to clear that up just as soon as we get back to be cabin. I don't know what you're doing, Jed, but I don't want any part of it."

"You're already part of it . . . and I need you." Jed stood up and stretched out his hand toward her. "And you didn't exaggerate," his voice soothed. "We *are* friends. Maybe this is what we needed to help us become close friends." He pulled her toward him. "How about it, Kathy?"

She felt his steel arms clamp around her, but she couldn't respond. Somehow he'd become a stranger.

"Marry me. We'd make a good team."

That's not a proposal. That's a business question, she thought, feeling suffocated in his grip. *No tenderness, no fireworks. It's all wrong.*

"Kathy?"

"I need some time to think." She put out her hands and firmly pressed him away. "This isn't quite the way I'd hoped for a proposal."

"Things don't always work out the way we plan them." Jed dropped his arms and took her hand. They started back toward the cabin. "Okay. You think about it—but even more, *do* something about that trip. It's very important. I can't explain, but I know I can trust you."

The porch light was on when they got back, casting a circle of light on the patio with Trevor in its center. He sat reading the newspaper at the picnic table.

"Where's Cynthia?" Kathy stepped into the circle and sat on the bench opposite him.

"Fixing a salad." He jerked a thumb toward the house.

Jed stayed in the shadows and lifted the lid on the barbeque. "The fire's ready."

Trevor folded one corner of the newspaper down and glanced questioningly over it in Jed's direction.

"Oh, I'm sorry." Kathy caught his look. "I forgot you two haven't met. Jed, this is Trevor Kingston. Trevor, Jed James."

The two men approached each other and stopped at the edge of the light. Trevor, standing tall and poised, extended his hand into the shadows. "Glad to meet you, Jed."

Jed momentarily clasped Trevor's hand in greeting, standing so that only his curly red hair was illuminated in the glowing beam. Each man sized the other up quickly, silently. Tension stretched the moment till the air snapped.

"Glad you're here," Trevor added after a moment.

"Thanks for inviting me."

"Any . . . friend of Kathy's is welcome." Trevor emphasized the word *friend* just enough to make Kathy color slightly and remember her vow to set the matter straight.

"Trevor," Kathy started, "I meant to tell you that Jed and I are—"

"I suppose she's told you I've asked her to marry me," Jed interrupted.

"Jed," Kathy gasped, "you know I—"

"No, she didn't tell me. Congratulations." Trevor seemed to freeze, then abruptly turned toward the cabin. "I'll see if Cynthia needs any help."

Throughout their meal, Kathy's disgust at Jed smoldered, permeating the air, punctuating the silences. Only Cynthia's endless chatter saved the evening. Even then her continual use of "Trevie" this and "Trevie" that grated on Kathy's nerves. She finally excused herself, blaming a headache.

Without turning on the bedroom light, Kathy softly slid open a window to allow the cool night air to freshen her room. Later, she sank gratefully into the comforts of the huge poster bed. At first the murmur of voices outside remained only a fringe sound. But as they grew louder, she couldn't help but listen.

"We're alone at last," Jed's voice brought Kathy's eyes wide open.

"Too bad Kathy had a headache," Cynthia's tone sounded sympathetic.

"I'm glad *you* are still here," his voice was low with meaning.

Soft, undefinable sounds blew in as the curtains moved in the breeze. Kathy thought about closing the window, but knew they would hear her. After those last words, she didn't want to be seen or heard.

The shock of Jed's words whirled through her mind. Why would he ask her to marry him, then immediately make a play for Cynthia? She sought and rejected several solutions.

First Trevor and Cynthia, and now Jed—they're all playing games. Kathy lay still, trying to think. *What's going on?*

"You live in Spokane?"

"Yes, out in the valley." Cynthia's voice was silky. "Do you ever get up there?"

"Not often. When do you have to go back?" Jed's tone was really saying, "I don't want you to leave, but . . ." Suddenly, Kathy knew what he was doing.

"Maybe tomorrow . . . or the next day," Cynthia responded. "I came to see Trevie, but he just didn't seem too pleased. Must be all the work he's doing. It's spoiling his vacation."

"I know. A man needs to relax once in a while, take a night off now and then."

"Like tonight?" Cynthia must have been right up against the screen for her voice to carry so far and still be so low.

"Yes, like tonight." Jed hesitated, then sounding reluctant asked, "Will Kathy be flying you back when you go?"

"Trevie said she could take me anytime. In fact, I have a party invitation for tomorrow night at Coeur d'Alene, but I was going to skip it."

"Why skip it?" Jed's question confirmed Kathy's suspicion. "After this fiasco tonight, you could probably use a few laughs. Besides, you've got a magic carpet that will take you directly to Idaho unless you think you have to stop in Spokane first."

"Maybe you're right. I'll ask Trevie in the morning." Cynthia seemed eager to follow Jed's suggestion. "That'll give me all day here to relax before I go to the party. I wouldn't have to go home first. I always travel prepared for a party . . . if you know what I mean," she added in a muffled voice after a few moments of silence.

Not wanting to hear any more, Kathy pulled her pillow over her head. When she lifted it a few minutes later to see if they were gone, she heard one last snatch of conversation. "Meet me at the bronze foundry at two," Jed said. "There's some art you really shouldn't miss."

Their voices drifted off, and Kathy wondered if they were going on a moonlight walk. *Maybe down the same path we took earlier.* She thought about Jed's proposal and felt a sudden emptiness inside, as though she'd lost a friend. And then, turning a damp cheek to her pillow, she realized that indeed she had lost a very dear friend—but his hair wasn't red.

"God," she whispered into the pillow, "please help me clear up this mess."

———————

At the first hint of dawn, Kathy rolled out of the tangled sheets and shrugged into jeans and a sweatshirt. She'd had little sleep, and a walk on the mountain sounded inviting.

Outside she stepped silently across the empty patio, skirted Trevor's camper, and found the path leading up the side of the hill. So many things pressed her mind for attention that she didn't notice the dampness until a wet branch slapped her back to reality.

She glanced at the sky and saw low, dark clouds layered against a higher gray overcast. Stepping off the path, she found some dry pine needles and scooped them together beneath their mother tree. Nestling in their softness, she leaned back against the pine trunk, lost again in thought.

The conversation between Jed and Cynthia pounded through her brain. For the millionth time she wondered, *Why?*

Why did he propose to me like that—so coldly? What was so important about that package that he wouldn't talk about it? She closed her eyes and recalled the way Jed had effectively maneuvered Cynthia into flying back to the Spokane area. *I know he did it so I could take his package.*

Well, I may have to fly her to her party, she determined, *but I won't take that package.* Her eyes stung as she fought for control. *He can just get someone else to meet that creepy Frank!*

A soft splattering on the leaves announced the beginning of rain. She sighed aloud, thinking of Trevor. Tears trickled down her face as a lonely aching swept her heart. She knew he didn't love her. Time stretched endlessly in front of her as she thought of the hours she would have to spend near him. Every moment would have to be guarded lest she slip and he discover her feelings for him.

"God," she whispered out loud, knowing He would hear her. "Will it never end?"

"All things come to an end!"

Kathy's eyes flew open at the familiar deep voice. "Trevor! What . . . what are you doing here?"

"I might ask you the same." He sank down on a rock facing her. "I've been watching you for quite a while—from over there." He pointed to a secluded cove above the path. "It's one of my favorite places to meditate." He indicated a small black book in his shirt pocket. It looked suspiciously like a New Testament.

"I didn't know you were here," she apologized. "If you'd like, I'll leave." She leaned forward and started to raise up.

"Stay. Please?" He put out a hand and pressed her shoulder lightly, so she sank back into the nest. "What's wrong?" He touched the tears on her cheek, his fingers sending tremors of fire across her skin. "For a woman who has just gotten engaged, you don't seem too happy. Is there anything I can do?"

"No, I . . ." She shook her head slowly, then decided to try and clear up one problem, if she could. "That is, I'm not engaged. At least, I don't think I am."

"You're not making much sense."

"I don't know why Jed said that to you last night." She choked over the words, but was relieved that she could tell him the truth. "He had no right to say that."

"But he *did* ask you to marry him?" Trevor's voice was low and clear.

"Yes," Kathy pulled away and ducked her head.

"Did you refuse him?" She had to strain to hear his words.

Kathy slowly shook her head and an involuntary tremor convulsed her shoulders.

"But if you said *yes*, then you're engaged!" Trevor stood

up and turned away from her. The hem of his jeans were damp where he'd brushed against some wet undergrowth.

"I didn't say yes," Kathy denied, looking down at her hands and nervously playing with some pine needles. "Oh, what's the use!" She threw them down and stood up too. "You wouldn't understand . . . or even believe me."

"If you didn't say yes and you didn't say no, just what *did* you say to him?" Trevor had turned again and was moving close to her. His nearness made her heart beat faster. Her eyelashes fluttered down to mask her feelings.

"It was all wrong. I . . . I just said I needed time to think." Her breath came too quickly, but he didn't seem to notice.

"What's the matter? Didn't he go down on bended knee?" There was a mocking tone to his words. "What does a man need to do to ask you to marry him?"

"Nothing—I mean . . . I'm just so confused."

"Well, just be sure that you love him before you accept."

Kathy looked up and saw the cold mask on Trevor's face again. "That's just it. I *don't* love him . . . or I thought I did once, but we were just friends. And now, even that's gone."

"Why? If he loves you, he'll keep trying."

"No." She heaved a deep sigh. "He wants me to do a favor for him, and I can't . . . or that is, I won't."

"What kind of favor?" There was no mistaking the instant change in Trevor's voice. The coldness was gone, and he was staring intently into her eyes.

"Not what you're thinking!" She turned red in spite of the tenseness of their conversation. "It isn't important," she shrugged, trying to back off from his intense questions.

"Kathy," his voice was firm as he reached out to touch her chin. "This favor could be *very* important. Tell me about it." There was such a controlled command in his tone that the whole thing spilled out before she could stop herself. "I don't care what he says," she finished. "I wouldn't meet that guy Frank again for anything!" She shivered again.

"Come on." He put his arm around her shoulders. "You need a cup of coffee, and I know a special place."

Kathy trembled again at his touch and steeled herself against his nearness. It would be so easy just to lean back on his strong arms.

Dear God, she breathed a silent prayer heavenward, *please give me strength and guidance for this day.*

"Cold?"

"A little, I guess." Dampness penetrated her clothes as she moved out onto the trail beside him. "I didn't know it was raining when I started out this morning."

"That was obvious! You weren't paying much attention to anything when I saw you." Trevor kept his hand on her shoulder even when she had to move in front of him on the narrow path. "Let's follow the stream downhill. It's shorter."

They edged quietly down the mountain, listening to muffled sounds of music drifting in the air. Pausing, Kathy looked up at Trevor, questioning the music.

"The church camp," he nodded toward some nearby buildings. "The children have been here all week. I've stopped several times to hear them sing."

Kathy nodded an acknowledgment. She'd never approached the camp from this angle before. In her mind, she could see the children lined up on wooden benches as they sang joyfully, Professor Strauss in front of them.

13

"Come over here by this tree." Trevor drew her under its shelter from the rain. Opening his heavy jacket, he wrapped her next to his chest. "This'll keep you warm while we listen."

Kathy's cheeks blushed a deep pink and she fought an urge to pull away from him. Then, realizing he was being kind, she relaxed slowly with the soothing music and the warmth of his body. Admittedly she was puzzled at this display of tender concern, so opposite from his coldness last night.

So many moods, she thought, feeling his chin rest on the top of her head. *If I were married to him, I'd never be bored. I'd never know which Trevor would walk through the door.* Then, noticing just how far her thoughts had taken her, she blushed furiously again and hoped he wouldn't notice.

To help clear her mind, Kathy concentrated on her last talk with Professor Strauss. She knew he would probably lead the children in a time of devotions as soon as their song service was over.

The children's voices rose in song, their words penetrating her fog.

Let God do it. Trust and obey.
Let God do it. He knows the way.

Their voices were strong, sure that the message was true. Kathy sensed her confidence in God pushing through her confusion. God knew the way out of the chaos she was feeling right now. All this mix-up with Jed, her love for Trevor, Trevor's love for Cynthia—the whole mess was pretty unusual. She needed His guidance now more than ever.

"He knows the way." Their voices slowed as the melody ended.

Trevor's arms tightened around her ever so slightly, and he sighed. "Ready?" He glanced at his watch as he allowed her to move out from his warmth. "If we hurry, we'll be there just in time."

"Where? In time for what?" Kathy fell into step beside him on the trail again.

"You'll see," he answered with a mysterious smile. At the end of the trail he led her across the creek and into a tiny restaurant labeled *Vali's*.

Kathy sank back into her chair in the corner of the tiny Bavarian restaurant as she waited for Trevor to bring their coffee. The small room was crowded with vacationers pushing toward the front counter, where a diminutive woman with salt-and-pepper hair bantered with the customers.

"Try these." He handed her a long, twisted donut, sprinkled with cinnamon and sugar. "They were baked this morning." He sat down beside her and placed cups of steaming coffee on the table.

"Mmmm," Kathy sank her teeth into the soft, warm dough. "Heavenly." She washed it down with a strong draught of coffee.

"We had to time it just right," Trevor explained. "Maggie opens the door at nine." He jerked a thumb at the lady behind the counter. "And when the morning's batch of goodies are gone, they close. It's that simple," he said between large bites. "Usually everything's sold in less than an hour. Want another one?"

"I shouldn't, but they're so good." Kathy wiped sugar

and cinnamon granules from the edges of her mouth with a napkin.

"Glutton," he teased and got up to buy two more. When he came back, he poured more coffee, filling both cups to the rim.

Kathy drank hers gratefully, letting the warmth permeate her whole body.

"Kathy," Trevor pushed his chair back in the crowded room and stretched his legs. "I'm going to ask you to do something you don't want to do."

She drained her cup and placed it back in its saucer, searching his face.

"Whatever Jed asks you to do—take a package, meet Frank, whatever—just agree. Then tell me."

"Why?" She twisted her cup nervously. "Trevor, what's going on? I feel as if everyone's playing games and no one is telling me the truth."

"This isn't the time or the place to explain," he shook his head and traced the edge of his napkin with strong fingers. "In fact, it would be better if you didn't know. Just trust me, please?"

"That's what Jed said, too." Kathy's eyes followed his hands, and just for a second she had the urge to reach out and touch his fingers. "I don't like it. Maybe you should get another pilot."

"Don't leave, Kathy. I need you."

"You two must have the same scriptwriter." Kathy shook her head slowly, remembering Jed's words in the darkening forest.

"What?" His eyes snapped to meet hers.

"Oh, nothing." She twirled her cup absently. Trevor and Jed had both said the same thing: *Trust me. I need you.* Which one should she trust?

She'd known Jed the longest. Their hours together, the fun they'd shared over the last few years, seemed a lifetime ago. Right now it was difficult to picture him with his curly red hair and laughing green eyes. Last night he had become a stranger.

And there was Trevor. He really *was* a stranger. Yet of the two, Kathy wanted to trust him the most. How had she managed to fall in love with this tall, dark-haired man so quickly? And because of that love, even unreturned, she was willing to trust him more than Jed. She sighed, no closer to an answer than she'd been before. *Lord, I really need your guidance.* She sent a silent prayer toward heaven. *You have said you can guide us in any situation if we ask you. So I'm asking. Please show me the way.*

"Well, will you?"

"Will I what?" Kathy looked up, startled at his interruption of her thoughts.

"You've been a long way off. Trying to make up your mind, right?" Trevor was leaning forward, one elbow on the table, the other hand braced on his knee. He was so powerful, so magnetic. "Will you trust me?"

"If ever I needed divine guidance, it's now." She gazed at him intently. "The truth is, I don't know which one of you to believe. The only thing I can promise is that I won't leave. My dad wanted me here, and as far as flying goes, I'll do whatever you ask. The rest will have to work itself out somehow."

"God knows the way." Trevor spoke so softly she almost didn't hear him.

"What?"

"The song . . . on the mountain." His voice was gentle. "The children sang those words. Didn't you hear them?"

"Of couse, and I do trust Him—at least I try to. I certainly can't rely on myself for this answer." She smiled slowly, feeling more lighthearted than she'd felt all morning.

"Come on," Trevor stood up, amazed at the transformation on her face. "Let's get back to the cabin and see what's happening."

Later, dressed in jeans and a peach blouse, Kathy brushed her hair carefully. It was very fine and, freshly washed from her shower, it shone honey gold in the soft lustre of her room.

In the mirror she could see the wall behind her. Shafts of morning sun crept upward. One beam touched the lone picture and gave the angel an unearthly glow as she hovered to protect the children. Evidently the clouds were breaking up outside, allowing the summer sun to wash away the earlier gloom.

Kathy sauntered over to the window and peered toward the sky. "Just as I thought: breaks in the overcast," she referred to the clouds. "If I have to fly Cynthia home, at least I'll be able to get off the ground." She was still staring at the widening gaps in the clouds when a knock sounded at her door.

"Kathy?" Trevor tried the knob, then opened the door slightly.

"You *do* have a habit of walking in!" Kathy couldn't help but smile at the chagrined look on his face. "Doesn't anyone ever complain?"

"But it wasn't locked," he protested, an answering smile spreading across his face.

"Never mind," she laughed. "What did you want?"

"You were right about last night." Trevor moved over to the window beside her. He had changed into white trousers and a blue shirt that matched his eyes. "Cynthia has asked if you'll fly her to Coeur d'Alene late this afternoon. I checked the weather with Flight Service, and everything looks okay. There'll be a few cumulus over the mountains later, but I think you can avoid them."

Kathy raised an eyebrow at his use of the word *cumulus*. Most nonpilots just called them clouds. "You really have flown a lot. You've picked up all the right terms."

Seeming to ignore her comment, he added, "Would you go with me to that foundry now?"

A frown flicked across her eyes. "Sure, but why?"

"You said Jed asked Cynthia to meet him there at two o'clock." He referred to all the details she'd told him on the mountain. "I'd like to see it before they get there."

Driving back toward town along the edge of the lake, Kathy watched the boats loaded with hopeful fishermen. There were even a few brave souls on paddleboats enjoying the midday respite from the earlier rain.

"Looks like fun, doesn't it?" Trevor followed her gaze. "Maybe you and I can do that one of these days, but right now it's all work."

"Not much of a vacation for you, is it?" Kathy glanced at him.

"I thrive on hard work." He shrugged. "Besides, there were a few peaceful moments yesterday, or had you forgotten?"

Thinking of their trip on the gondola, Kathy smiled and ran her fingers through her hair. "No, I haven't forgotten."

Her mind went back to the horse and butterfly cup as she wondered about the promise it held. She was about to voice her thoughts when Trevor turned the car onto a side road and parked in front of the foundry.

"I've never been here before," she commented, stepping out of the car and taking in the long, low building.

"There has been a recent influx of artists in the valley, so the foundry was built to accommodate them." Trevor opened the door. "As their work became known, other artists started sending their art here to be cast. It's grown into quite a respectable business."

"Are we looking for anything special?" Kathy noted that her watch said one o'clock.

"No, just absorb everything you can." Trevor held the

door for her. "We'll talk about it later."

Inside, a petite woman with short gray hair greeted them. "Would you like a tour?" She smiled openly. "We're always happy to have visitors."

Kathy waited while her eyes adjusted to the dim interior. Along one wall a low shelf held several large metal bronzes of Indians, cowboys on horses, and an enormous eagle. On the floor there were a number of other bronze art castings.

"They're beautiful." Kathy examined the eagle. "I've never paid much attention to bronzes. Are they expensive?"

"That one sells for around thirty thousand," the woman answered.

"Oh," Kathy gasped, "I knew art was expensive, but I had no idea—"

"It's because they're made in very limited editions," Trevor explained.

"The artist creates an original sculpture," the guide spoke behind them, "like this one of an owl. Then we make a mold of it at the foundry and pour a limited number of bronzes. Each one is numbered," she turned the bronze and pointed to the number twenty-six on its base. "Then the mold is returned to the artist so it can be destroyed."

"So that's what keeps the price so high." Kathy traced the feathers on a bronze owl with her fingertips.

"That and the artist's reputation," nodded the guide. "And the public's demand. For example, if there are only thirty bronzes and fifty people want one, the price eventually climbs to whatever the highest bidder will pay."

"Could we see how they're made?" The feathers on the owl were so detailed, Kathy was curious.

"The process begins in here," the guide opened a door into a side room with racks of wax chunks that at first seemed to be misshapen globs. At several tables, workers bent over delicate pieces, working with dentist's tools.

The smell of hot wax stung Kathy's nostrils and brought tears to her eyes.

"Those are the molds." The guide pointed to pink and gray hollow chunks on the floor. "When they're filled with hot wax, these pieces are produced." She pointed to the racks beside her. "Then the workers put them together to form the second stage of the bronze process."

"Why are they using such small tools?" Kathy nodded toward a dental pick the nearest woman was holding.

"They are restoring the lines or details that are sometimes lost or damaged during the first molding. Otherwise, when the bronze is actually cast, the final product might not be exactly like the original."

Moving through some swinging doors, the guide led them into a large warehouse-type room. "After the second stage is completed, those figures are dipped into a slurry to make a second mold. When that is dry, they're brought in here."

Kathy felt Trevor touch her shoulder. "They are those cement-looking things." He pointed to a shelf of grotesquely shaped chunks.

"You've been here before?" Kathy looked up at him.

"A couple of times," he nodded.

"Over there," the guide continued, pointing toward two men, "hot bronze is poured into the second mold after the wax is melted out. It's called the lost wax method."

Kathy was fascinated as she watched them carefully handling molten bronze, turning the molds over and over.

"When those are done"—the guide took them through another set of swinging doors—"they are brought in here where the pieces are reassembled by metalworkers."

"What is that man doing?" Kathy indicated one man wearing a mask and bent over a bronze horse.

"He's adding color," the guide explained. "By using a variety of acids, different colors or patinas can be achieved.

Notice this piece." She pointed to a finished horse just like the one he was working on. "The mane and tail are black, but the horse is golden. Some artists prefer to use paint rather than acid for color.

"Once the patina process is finished, the bronze is coated with wax to make it shine." The guide ushered them back into the first room.

After thanking the guide for their tour, Trevor paused again beside the finished bronzes for a moment before leading Kathy outside.

Blinking in the bright sunlight, Kathy noticed the sky was clearer. "If it's okay with you"—she looked around, noticing that they were close to the airport—"I'd like to check on the plane."

"I'll drive you out there." Trevor opened the car door for her. "Then when you're through maybe we can catch a bite to eat. This way we won't risk meeting Jed and Cynthia here at the foundry."

"That was all very interesting, but I didn't see anything unusual. Of course, it was all so new I probably wouldn't have recognized anything odd if it had been there." She climbed into the car. "I still don't understand—but I'm not asking any questions," Kathy hurried to add, seeing his quick frown. "Like a lamb led to the slaughter, I'll just follow along."

It only took a few minutes to drive to the airport, and Kathy immediately called Flight Service. Trevor's "few cumulus over the mountains" wasn't the kind of in-depth weather briefing she needed. She deliberately lingered over the preflight procedures, checking and double-checking everything on the plane. When enough time had passed, they drove back to town.

14

"*I* wish I had the horse cup to pour your milk shake into." Trevor handed Kathy her hamburger and shoved the paper-contained drink toward her when they were back at the restaurant.

"That cup again." Kathy poked her straw into the thick chocolate-marshmallow shake. "Why don't you just come out and tell me what your secret is?"

"Can't just yet." Trevor swallowed a bite of hamburger. "But I just wanted to keep reminding you that the message is there. Don't forget."

They ate silently. Trevor seemed to withdraw from her, and Kathy puzzled over the mystery of the cup. Whatever it was, the message eluded her.

"Tell me about yourself." Kathy started fishing for information. If there was a message, she'd need some clues. Besides, these past weeks had really piqued her curiousity about him.

"Not much to tell." Trevor leaned back in his chair. "What do you want to know?"

"Well, I see a man who is so married to his job he can't even take a proper vacation." Kathy let her eyes slide carefully over his features—straight nose, blue eyes, and thick brown hair. "Yet there's another Trevor—one who seems completely at home in the mountains—like this morning."

"So?"

"So . . . which one is the real Trevor Kingston?"

"Both. I was raised in the mountains on a ranch." He leaned both elbows on the table, bringing him uncomfortably close to her. "But a man needs a job, so it was off to the big city. I come back whenever I can."

"You can take the man out of the mountains, but you can't take the mountains out of the man?" Kathy poked at the sesame seeds that had fallen off her hamburger bun.

"Something like that," he nodded. "I miss the quiet."

"I know what you mean." She looked up and caught a faraway gleam in his eye. "Watching the deer whisper past me on the trail this morning made me wish I never had to go back. I used to dream about the comfort of the hills when I was in college."

"You surprise me." Trevor was examining her face closely. "When I first met you, I'd have sworn you were one of those fiesty, militant women. You know the kind—out to conquer the 'man's' world. Don't get me wrong"—he saw her quick intake of breath—"I like spunky women."

"It's just that I've seen two women, too," he went on. "There's the efficient one in the air who flies with precision. I'd expect her to be aiming for transoceanic flying. But then I find a woman who'd rather hike in the rain than lollygag in bed. One who waits for a squirrel to eat from her hand. To repeat a question I just heard, which one is the real Kathy Evans?"

"I'm afraid my temper does get out of hand once in a while." Kathy grinned impishly as she remembered her first meeting with him. "Mom and Peggy are both so quiet and even-tempered. I guess I'm a crazy blend. I want things to be right, and when they aren't, I get all worked up. Dad's like that."

"You're like your dad in a lot of ways."

"You know him?" Surprised, Kathy looked up from the straw she'd been twisting.

"I . . . that is"—Trevor squirmed a bit—"of course. I

met him in Pendleton when I arranged for our first flight. I told him I'd be in La Grande in a week and I'd need transportation to the lake."

"Was Cynthia with you when you met my dad?" She wasn't any closer to solving his mystery.

The slow red that tinged his cheekbones made Kathy think she'd hit on something important.

"What makes you ask?" he evaded.

"Oh, she seems such an important part of your life—I'm using her cabin, she flies down here for your vacation. I just thought—oh no!" Kathy groaned, breaking off as a very familiar woman opened the restaurant door.

"Trevie! I just knew you'd be here somewhere when I saw your car outside." Cynthia's high voice trilled across the restaurant. Her black hair was caught back coyly from her face with a blue scarf. Her sleeveless top, worn over white shorts, matched the blue scarf—or at least what little there was of it matched.

Didn't waste any fabric on that one, Kathy thought, *and both these men are drooling!* Jed had walked in behind Cynthia, his green eyes barely taking in Kathy and Trevor before returning to linger on Cynthia.

"Jed's just given me a delightful tour of that little foundry." Cynthia gave him a lingering liquid glance. "But now I'm anxious to get up north for the party. How soon can we leave?"

"That's up to Kathy." Trevor rose from his chair.

"Anytime," Kathy muttered, wishing she could plan a parachute drop over the mountains for a certain black-haired woman—minus the chute! "Weather looks passable, till evening anyway."

"I'll need to change my clothes." Cynthia patted her shorts, and both men automatically followed the movement of her hands. "Can you take me back to the cabin?"

Kathy ground her teeth to keep silent at the way the

other woman was playing up to both men. If she said a single word, they'd all know how jealous she was.

"Kathy, you don't need to go back to the cabin too, do you?" Jed tore his eyes away and turned toward Kathy. "I mean, why don't you come out to the airport with me? There are a few things we need to talk about . . . alone." He reached out and grasped her wrist, pulling her toward him.

"The lovebirds," Cynthia cooed, a smirk on her face. "I'd almost forgotten he proposed to her last night."

"I didn't forget," Trevor mumbled, his knuckles white as he gripped the back of the chair beside him. "But it's a good idea. Kathy, you go with Jed. I'll take Cynthia back to the cabin for her suitcases." He stood up and roughly shoved his chair aside. "We'll meet you at the plane in an hour, okay?"

"That's fine." Kathy kept a bland mask on her face. It wouldn't do to let her emotions show. Jed was holding her wrist so tightly, she knew he didn't want her to disagree.

He was silent as they bounced along in his Jeep during the short distance to the airport. But the sharp turn at the end of the road sent gravel scattering and revealed Jed's intense feelings.

"Have you decided about us?" he asked gruffly, waiting for her to climb out and join him on the gravel.

"You mean the proposal? I . . . I . . . think we'd better wait on that one, Jed." Kathy wished with all her heart that Trevor were here. Whatever friendship she'd had with Jed had died last night outside her window, and now she was wary of him.

"Whatever you say," Jed shrugged. "But we'll have to hurry. There's lot's to do before they get back." He pulled her along with him toward the mechanic's shop.

"What do you mean, *lots to do*? I've already preflighted the plane."

"Get that screwdriver"—Jed pointed to his workbench—"while I put these on." He pulled on grease-streaked coveralls. "There's a small box in the pickup. Get it for me. It isn't heavy."

"But, Jed . . ." Kathy had to run to keep up with him as he crossed to where her airplane was parked. "I don't—"

"You don't have a choice," he snapped. "Now unlock the baggage area and keep quiet."

When she brought the box, she watched him shove it into the tail section. Then he neatly placed a fitted shield in front of it, fastening it into place with screws in newly formed holes. She wanted to ask when he'd made the shield and created the screw holes—it was all so perfectly fitted. But something in his manner made her keep quiet. When he was finished, no one would have suspected there was a false panel in the back.

"Now, after you deliver Cynthia to the Coeur d'Alene airport, go someplace for a cup of coffee." Jed wiped his hands on a faded red rag and slipped the screwdriver into his back pocket. "Stay there for at least an hour."

"But, Jed, I don't want to do this," she protested, searching wildly for a way to untangle this mess without antagonizing him.

Suddenly Jed grabbed her and pulled her against him. His mouth came down hard on hers, his arms pinning her firmly against the plane. His kiss was harsh, lasting a long time.

At first she'd been too shocked to struggle, then it had been too late. When he pulled back from her, she gulped for air, then spat out, "Is that how you treated Cynthia last night?"

Shock showed briefly on Jed's face. "Jealous?" A slow sardonic smile spread across his mouth. "Now that's what I call a woman. You could learn a lot from her."

He still held her clamped against him. "Maybe this'll make you change your mind about marrying me." He started to tilt her face toward him again when the sound of tires on gravel made him pause. Reluctantly he released her. "Well, if they saw anything, it'll just add to our image. Now, keep your mouth shut and do as I say. If you tell anyone, you'll pay for the rest of your life!"

Trevor and Cynthia approached the plane with only one small bag.

"I decided to travel light," Cynthia quipped. "This way I'll have an excuse to come back for my other things." She slid a provocative glance at Jed to imply far more than just her suitcases.

Still shaken by Jed's treatment, Kathy was nervous as they taxied out. With Trevor in the seat beside her and Cynthia in the back, she felt a tension in the airplane that she'd never known before. As they stopped to do the flight run-up, Trevor leaned close to her.

"What did he ask you to do?" His voice was low, but Kathy felt the authority. "Is there a package on board?"

"Yes," she nodded without pausing in her procedure, knowing Jed would wonder if she took even a few seconds longer at this normal task. "It's in a false compartment in the tail," Kathy whispered, checking both mags.

"What were your instructions?"

"Can I tell you after we're airborne? I don't think we should delay at this point." Kathy shuddered as she remembered Jed's final instructions.

At Trevor's nod, she moved into place on the runway, spoke her intentions into the microphone, and thrust the throttle all the way forward. A few minutes later, when she'd established her airborne course, she broke the silence.

"Trevor, please tell me what's going on." Kathy scanned her panel again and glanced over at him. "I don't want to do this—in fact, I won't until I know more."

Trevor sighed, looked into the backseat at Cynthia, and seemed to make a decision. "Tell me your instructions, then maybe I can answer at least part of your questions."

Kathy kept her eyes out the window, chosing to go around a cloud rather than through it. "After Cynthia gets out in Coeur d'Alene, I'm to leave the airplane alone for about an hour."

"So they can remove the package." Trevor nodded. "That makes sense. Well, I want to know what's in the package first. *Then* you can deliver it."

"Trevor . . ." Cynthia leaned forward, her voice pitched much more moderately and businesslike than Kathy had ever heard before. "Let's land at Lewiston. You can check the package, and I'll call ahead."

"Trevor?" Kathy raised her eyebrow. "What happened to *Trevie*?" She pitched her voice high in a mimic of Cynthia's former tone.

"It's always been just Trevor." Cynthia touched Kathy's shoulder. "Except for this time." Her newly moderated voice lacked its usual irritation. "He wouldn't ever let me get away with calling him *Trevie* before."

Kathy could hardly concentrate on flying—too many thoughts pelted her brain. "You promised some explanations," she prompted.

"Plan a course for Lewiston," Trevor reminded her.

With one hand on the controls, Kathy flipped some switches, checked her wind drift, and used her flight calculator. "We've picked up a tail wind," she announced, making a slight course correction. "All set for Lewiston. Now . . . about that explanation."

"Okay," Trevor sighed again. "I guess you deserve something. What do you want to know?"

"First of all," Kathy answered. "Who are you?"

"I thought I'd already told you."

"You're evading the question."

"All right. You already know I'm an insurance investigator, but Cynthia is an undercover police agent." He turned in his seat to include the other woman. "We're on the track of some stolen—or rather, reproduced—art objects."

"Like those things we saw at the foundry today?"

"Yes," Cynthia joined the conversation. "In fact, we're pretty sure that whatever is in your package probably came from there."

Lewiston control tower cut into their conversation, and they all waited until the radio was quiet again.

"So Jed's been having me transport stolen art . . . first that package in La Grande the day I met you, Trevor. And then the one Frank sent that awful night in Spokane."

"I'm sorry . . ." Cynthia now sounded so different from the lightheaded socialite that Kathy could hardly believe they were the same person. "I guess it's pretty hard for you to take. Maybe we shouldn't have told you in the air like this."

"I-I'm fine." Kathy's voice caught a little because she just realized that Trevor still hadn't explained his personal relationship with Cynthia. And this new side to Cynthia's personality certainly made her into the kind of woman Trevor would want—maybe already had.

Kathy shuddered at a new thought. Maybe they were married—that would explain a lot. Firmly she pushed aside this train of thought. It was time to land in Lewiston, and flying took all her concentration.

"Seat belts fastened?" She glanced quickly at each passenger, then pushed the fuel mixture to *Full/Rich*, and eased the throttle back. Moments later they landed and taxied to the terminal.

Trevor jumped out first, and Cynthia scrambled out of the backseat. "I'll be right back," she called, hurrying toward the terminal.

"Now, show me that false shield." Trevor moved around to the luggage compartment.

Kathy opened the baggage area and pointed to the newly installed shield. "You'll need a Phillips screwdriver. I've got one in my toolbox." She rummaged under the seat and pulled out a flat plastic container.

In a few minutes, Trevor had removed the shield and pulled the box out. First he examined the package, and then smiled, pulling out his pocket knife. "This'll be easy."

At last the package lay open at their feet. Kathy stared at its contents. Finally she bent down and ran her fingers over the bronze feathers of the owl. Had it only been a few hours since she'd touched these same bronze feathers in the foundry in Joseph? Slowly she withdrew her hand, tears springing to her eyes.

Trevor, kneeling over the box, looked up to see why she was so quiet. Noting the whiteness that made her hazel eyes seem to dominate her delicate face, he stood up. "I think you'd better sit down." He put his arm around her for support. "This has been more of a shock than I thought."

Kathy nodded, dropping to the ground. More tears trickled down her face as she thought about Jed. "I guess I'd hoped that we were wrong . . . that we'd find a part for an airplane in that box." A small sob caught and convulsed her shoulders.

"You also asked for divine guidance this morning, remember?" Trevor sat beside her and pulled her gently against his chest. "It's better for you to learn this now than after you married him."

Quietly Kathy pressed her face into the softness of his shirt, breathing deeply to control her sobs. *If this is God's way of giving guidance,* she shuddered, *it sure hurts.* It wasn't until Cynthia's voice broke the stillness that Kathy remembered the strength she'd been drawing from Trevor might belong to the other woman.

"What's happening?" Cynthia came up behind them.

"She's had a terrible shock." Trevor squeezed Kathy's

shoulders gently as she pulled away from him.

"I'll . . . I'll . . . be fine." Kathy dabbed at her eyes with the handkerchief Trevor gave her.

"Check that box." Trevor indicated the open package and stood up. "Have you seen this one before?"

"No, it's a new bronze—at least new to me." Cynthia studied the owl carefully.

"It, or one like it, was at the foundry today." Kathy joined them. Her knees were still a bit wobbly. "Don't you remember, Trevor?"

"On the floor . . . near the eagle, right?"

"It wasn't there when Jed and I went through." Cynthia petted the bronze owl absently.

"Sure?" Trevor pushed for clarity.

"Absolutely."

"The number," Kathy remembered. "Check the number. It was twenty-six."

Trevor lifted the bronze and confirmed, "Right there . . . number twenty-six."

"Now what?" Kathy felt a little stronger, but wished she had a cup of coffee.

"Now I'll put it back and we deliver it. Step back, Kathy, so Cynthia can photograph it." He moved out of the way, too, as Cynthia snapped a pocket camera.

"But why . . . why deliver it?" Kathy just wanted to turn it all over to the police and get away.

"We have to stop them in the act of receiving stolen goods." Trevor carefully replaced the box and its wrappings exactly as they had been. "You made contact?" he asked Cynthia.

"They'll be waiting when we land. I'll keep up the act of going to a party, and you two get a cup of coffee. Just be sure the baggage door is left unlocked." She climbed back into the airplane and fastened her seat belt.

Kathy's hands were still shaking a bit as she and Trevor

took their places in the front after they'd replaced the box and shield. "I'm having a little trouble adjusting to this new Cynthia," she raised an eyebrow at the other woman and added a quick smile. "You're very different than I thought you were."

"I had to be that way." Cynthia, too, smiled warmly. "We've been on to Jed's activities for a while, but we weren't sure about how you fit into his plans. If he didn't use you, *I* needed to be available. A sexy woman is usually the fastest way to get a man's attention, and I didn't have much time."

"You didn't need much time." Kathy managed a small laugh. "That outfit you were wearing this afternoon was quite powerful." As she eased the throttle forward, Kathy glanced at Trevor. A slow tinge of red touched his cheekbones, and she wondered why. *If she's his girlfriend . . . or wife,* Kathy amended, *he probably hated having her throw herself at another man like that.*

Kathy dropped all thoughts except the business of flying. The sky needed her full attention.

15

The clouds quickly formed a layer beneath them, and Kathy kept carefully above the billowing masses. Once or twice she caught Trevor openly watching her.

"Is something bothering you?" Kathy had caught his frank scrutiny again. "If it's the clouds, don't worry, we'll stay above them until the last minute possible."

"Not the clouds." Trevor leaned a little closer. "It's you. Are you sure you're up to all this flying?"

"Oh, I should have thought—of course you're worried. I'm fine." She gave him a reassuring smile. "There isn't any danger because of my flying skills. If I'd thought I wasn't up to it, I'd never have left the ground at Lewiston. You don't need to worry. I'm a better pilot than that. I'd never knowingly risk a passenger's safety."

"If you're sure—because I could . . ." Trevor sat back in his seat.

"You could what?" Kathy frowned, completely baffled by his words.

"Oh . . . nothing. As long as you're sure."

Ahead the clouds had broken up somewhat and Kathy decided to get below them. "Everyone belted in? I'm going to descend here and make a long approach."

The quiet of the last leg of their flight had helped Kathy get a better perspective. She had regained an inner calmness because she knew that God was helping her to make a wrong situation right. It was wrong to steal, no matter who did it, and Kathy felt a satisfaction in correcting this wrong. And learning who Trevor and Cynthia really were gave her a sense of calmness, too.

I prayed for guidance on how to sort out this mess, she thought, *and I can now see which choices are right.* She glanced outside at the sky all around her. She felt so close to God when she was flying.

I know that you're there, God, and that you're helping me. Her thoughts switched from musing to talking to God. It was odd how she could silently talk so intensely to God and still be fully in control of flying, almost like someone was helping her.

Again she sensed the deep inner peace of knowing that God was completely in control. She could trust Him to show her which way was best.

"There isn't a restaurant on the field," Kathy commented as they landed and taxied, "but we can go to the pilot's lounge. Somebody can find us a cup of coffee—and I certainly need one."

"Nervous?" Trevor had retreated into his tense, business self, the one she'd met that first day.

"Yes." But it was more than nervousness, she just needed to get alone to think and to pray.

"Just don't look around," he cautioned. "Get Cynthia's bag like you normally would and leave the compartment unlocked. We'll all go into the building together."

Kathy tried to act casual. It sounded so easy, but she dropped her keys twice trying to open the baggage door. At last she unlocked it and removed Cynthia's bag, then carefully made sure the door was closed but unlocked.

Cynthia and Trevor had kept up a light chatter about her "party" and plans for returning to Joseph on Saturday. Kathy handed the bag to Cynthia and followed the other two into the Flight Service building.

They might be casual about this, she thought, keeping her

eyes on the Flight Service door, *but I feel as brittle as a rusted hinge—and about as useful!*

Inside, she sank gratefully onto an old couch and waited while Trevor found some coffee and brought her a cup. Cynthia used the telephone on the wall to call a friend to come and pick her up "for the party" in tones so high and loud no one could miss it.

After she hung up, Cynthia turned to Kathy and babbled, "Why don't you come to the party with me, Kathy? I know you'd be welcome. We could have such fun!" All the calm quietness of the efficient Cynthia was swallowed into an empty-headed party girl. "I know Trevie wouldn't mind, would you?" She turned a pleading, little girl face toward him.

"I don't think there's time, Cynthia," he frowned and glanced at his watch. "I really need to get back tonight." Then turning toward Kathy, he added, "You don't mind missing the party, do you?"

She looked from one to the other, knowing it was all an act. Somehow she had to join in, to make it look real. "Actually I'd love to go to the party, Cynthia, but since Trevor has to get back . . . and I really didn't come prepared—the right clothes, you know." She shrugged meaningfully. "But maybe next time. Maybe we could have a party out at the lake when you come back on Saturday."

Cynthia pretended to pout and would have protested when Kathy stood up, cutting her off. "Think I'll go in and check the weather while we wait for your friends to come." She started toward the door when Trevor intercepted her.

"We're not in that much of a hurry," his tone was light, but his grip on her arm was painful. His scowl brooked no discussion as he turned her back to the couch. "Stay put!" he ordered in a whisper as he shoved her down onto the cushion.

She nodded and rubbed the spot on her arm that would

be a purple bruise by tomorrow. Waiting was miserable work. Glancing at her watch, she realized they'd only been away from the plane for twenty minutes. An hour would be an eternity.

Five more minutes passed and Trevor strode swiftly to the outside door on the opposite side of the room. Opening it a crack, he slowly let it widen, then stood there with his back to the opening. "I'll check to see if Cynthia's ride is here," he spoke loudly so anyone outside the door could hear, "while you two powder your nose." He jerked a meaningful thumb toward the ladies room and stepped outside.

Cynthia ushered Kathy into the ladies room and shut the door, bolting it. The room was intended for only one person, so they were cramped.

"How long do we have to stay here?" Kathy murmured.

Cynthia turned on the water faucet before replying, "Until Trevor signals the all clear." She placed her purse on the edge of the sink and took out a small revolver. "Just in case," she explained, checking the gun over thoroughly.

They waited a few more minutes, then Cynthia turned the water off and leaned against the door, listening.

Silence.

Kathy fussed with her image in the mirror, combing her already combed honey gold hair and freshening her lipstick. She wanted to scream against the silence, or at least pace the floor. But she couldn't do either one.

Questions ricocheted through her mind. *Where is Trevor? Is he all right? Please, God, let him be safe.*

"You must be very special."

Kathy frowned, not sure she'd heard the soft words from Cynthia. She glanced at the other woman and saw a gentle smile in her eyes.

"What?"

"I said, you must be very special," Cynthia said quietly, just above a whisper. "Usually I'm out there in the thick of things." She pointed toward the closed door. "But this time," she shrugged, "I'm guarding you."

"Guarding me? I don't understand."

"Neither do I." Cynthia raised an eyebrow, "But Trevor said that either I guard you or he wouldn't go through with this delivery."

"That doesn't make sense." Kathy shook her head. "Jed just told me to stay away from the plane for an hour. He didn't indicate I'd be in any danger."

Now was as good a time as any to ask that all-important question. "Are you and Trevor—I mean . . ."

"Shh!" Cynthia stopped her with a gesture. There was a noise in the room outside, a sort of scraping.

"I'd give my eyeteeth to know what's—" Hearing more noise outside the door, Cynthia broke off, motioning Kathy to be quiet.

A knock on the door was accompanied by Trevor's voice. "Cynthia? Kathy? Come on out."

Cynthia unbolted the door, and the two women pushed out into the main room reeling as if they'd been released from prison. The three of them stood like statues, each examining the others, no one saying a word.

Finally Cynthia broke the tension. "Is everything okay?" She gave Trevor a hug with one arm, still brandishing the revolver in her free hand.

"It's all over," he nodded, his arm around her waist. "You can put that away now. And thanks."

Their eyes seemed to lock in an unspoken message, and Kathy turned away. The knot in her stomach felt like a giant steel pretzel.

"I'll just check the weather," she mumbled, not looking back at them, and opened the connecting door to Flight Service.

Her face was strained and her throat felt like strips of flypaper when she stepped into the next room. She forced her mind back to business and listened to the weather briefing. In another hour or so the front would be moved farther east and they'd have clear skies all the way back to Joseph.

Outside, the cooler evening air felt refreshing. *At least I didn't finish asking my question,* Kathy shook her head. *This way neither one of them knows how I feel about Trevor. I never meant to fall in love with a married man. At least now this is over and I can go home.* She took a deep breath and sighed, *and find something to do to make me forget.*

She turned toward the mountains, enjoying their stately beauty in the evening light. "Thank you, God," she whispered, "for answering my prayer. Thank you for keeping Trevor safe."

The airplane waited patiently at the end of the circular ramp. Kathy edged down the gentle slope to check things over. Everything looked normal, except the baggage door hung open. Otherwise, no one was in sight and nothing looked amiss.

"Maybe nothing really happened," Kathy mused out loud, reaching for the open compartment.

"Sorry to disappoint you," Trevor's deep voice filled the silence, "but take a look at that tail section."

Kathy jumped at his nearness, then realized the grass had muffled his approach. Bending down, she surveyed the baggage interior, noting the gaping hole where Jed's shield had been removed. The rug had been ripped and scratch marks showed how hasty someone had been to reach the package.

"Frank?" Kathy questioned, motioning toward all the debris.

"Yes," Trevor nodded, his dark hair gleaming in the evening light. "But we stopped him. By the way, his real name wasn't Frank. Frank and Jesse were just code names."

"And Jed?" Kathy couldn't help the little sob that caught her throat, so much had happened in these last few hours.

"No, Jed's name is real. It's just that they used his last name, James, to base their codes on."

"Oh," Kathy shook her head, struggling to remember that Jesse James, the outlaw, had a brother named Frank. "Is it okay if I clean up this stuff before we fly home?" At Trevor's nod she carefully picked up all the loose nuts, screws, and debris so nothing would bounce around and cause problems.

Methodically she locked the baggage door and started the usual preflight procedures: check the left strut, tire, and brake; test the left fuel tank for water or sediment; retest the baggage door; run fingers along the fuselage for loose rivets—suddenly she straightened up and stared. Trevor was on the other side of the airplane, about three check points ahead of her, doing exactly the same thing.

"What do you think you're doing?" Being interested in flying was one thing, but this was carrying it a bit too far!

"Preflighting," came Trevor's calm reply as he moved beyond the horizontal stabilizer checkpoint.

"Thank you for helping," Kathy swallowed hard and tried to be tactful, "but I can do it. Anyway, the pilot has to do it."

"Kathy," Trevor stopped exactly opposite her with only the narrow fuselage between them. "There are a few things we need to clear up. As you said, the *pilot* has to do the preflight check—and since *I'm* flying us home, I'll do it."

"B-but . . . I don't understand," Kathy stammered. If he was a pilot, why had he hired her? Although his admission did answer some nagging questions she'd had. She put a hand on the tail section to steady herself as she waited for his reply.

Trevor reached out and touched her hand on the tail, his strong fingers wrapped around her delicate ones. "This isn't the time to explain, but if you need to see my license . . ." When she nodded, he let go of her hand long enough to pull out his wallet and extract his license. "It shows that I'm not only a pilot—but even worse," he grinned triumphantly, "I hold a flight examiner's rating!"

"But . . . why did you need me?" Her voice shook.

Trevor replaced the license and his wallet and reached for her hand again. His touch sent tingles all over her skin. A light breeze blew her hair forward, and Trevor gently brushed it away from her face with his free hand.

"Naturally you have a lot of questions, but right now I'd like to get this bird in the air."

His tenderness brought color to her face, and suddenly Kathy remembered that he didn't belong to her—he belonged to Cynthia. She jerked her hand away from his grasp so sharply that Trevor froze, staring with a puzzled frown.

"What's the matter?"

"Oh . . . uh . . . nothing." Kathy put both hands behind her and stepped back from the airplane. "Where's Cynthia?"

"She went to pick up a basket of food for our trip back." The light was fading and Trevor continued talking as he finished checking the plane. "We don't have time to stop at Lewiston for supper. I want to be back in Joseph as quickly as possible. They'll have some statements for us to sign after Jed is picked up."

Kathy followed him, watching his practiced movements as he skillfully touched each vital checkpoint. Now she rested her head against the strut on the passenger side. In all the excitement, she'd forgotten that Jed would have to face the authorities. A shudder twisted down her spine, and Trevor strode swiftly to her side.

"I think you'd better sit down," he said. "You look pale."

"I'm fine." Kathy tried to back away from him. "It's just that today has been . . . a bit overwhelming."

"I said sit down!" Trevor scooped her up in his arms and deposited her in the front passenger seat. "Are you always this obstinate?" Without giving her a chance to answer, he fastened her seat belt firmly.

When he closed her door and walked swiftly back to the building, Kathy felt an even deeper sense of loss. In spite of herself, a tear squeezed out from one corner of her eye and trickled down her face. Absently she brushed it away, sighing loudly.

She leaned her head back on the seat and watched the darkness drop around her and forced herself to relax, to remember that God was there to help her.

A full ten minutes passed before Trevor came back and climbed in beside her. It felt strange to be sitting with him in this reversed position.

"That front is fully out of the way. We should have clear skies all night." Trevor handed her a large basket. "See if you can find me a cup of coffee in there." He closed his door and reached across Kathy to check the lock on her door.

"Where's Cynthia?" Kathy paused in the act of opening the basket when she realized he was preparing to leave. "Isn't she going with us?"

"With us?" Trevor echoed, puzzled. "No, of course not. Why should she?"

"But . . . I mean, wasn't that party of hers just a cover to provide a reason to fly up here? I mean, there wasn't really a party, was there?"

"The only party was the one we held at the tail of this airplane, and you women missed it." Trevor smiled wryly, inserting the key. "Cynthia's part is done."

16

They certainly have an unusual relationship, Kathy thought, digging for some cups. She balanced the Thermos between her knees and found a cup with a lid. She filled it and handed it to Trevor, trying to ignore the touch of his fingers as he accepted the cup.

"Is something bothering you?" Trevor asked between sips from the cup.

"No . . . of course not." She reached for another cup to fill for herself. "What? Where did this come from?" Kathy held up the familiar horse and butterfly cup.

Trevor put his own cup on the dashboard and took the cup from her hands. "Let me fill it," he said, reaching for the Thermos. "Back at the cabin I asked Cynthia to be sure to bring it. I'm afraid she was as puzzled about it as you are." He laughed and handed it back, brimming full of steaming coffee.

Kathy accepted the cup and took a tiny sip, savoring the aroma of fresh coffee. "When are you going to tell me what this means?"

"Tonight . . . when we get back. I—" he broke off, shifting in his seat to face her. "Kathy, I . . ." He ran a finger lightly across her arm in an unmistakable meaning.

"Trevor, don't." Kathy pulled away from his touch. "Think about Cynthia."

"Cynthia?" He nearly exploded, scowling darkly as she retreated from him. "What's Cynthia got to do with anything?" He turned back and grabbed his own cup. "Here, hold this while I get us airborne."

She took both cups and snapped the lid tightly on his, balancing her own carefully so it wouldn't spill.

"Cynthia," he muttered, shaking his head as they taxied to the run-up area. "I don't understand you."

"But . . . but she's your wife," Kathy protested. "Surely you don't think I'm the kind of woman who'd come between a husband and wife?"

"My wife?" Suddenly a whimsical smile flitted across his face. "My wife, huh?" He seemed lost in thought as he checked both mags and the carb heat. Satisfied that everything was at last air-ready, he called the unicom, "Departing runway one niner."

"Have a nice flight," was the response.

"Thank you, I will." Trevor was openly smiling as he replaced the microphone and shoved the throttle all the way in.

"So you think you're coming between my wife and me." Trevor had climbed to altitude and leveled off.

Kathy automatically handed him his coffee as though she'd done it a dozen times. "I guess I didn't mean it quite that way," she stammered.

During the run-up procedures she'd had time to think. Really he hadn't said anything that indicated how he felt about her. She'd only let her own feelings add too much meaning to his actions. Now she'd have to back off and cover her tracks. "Just what *did* you mean?" Trevor switched on the autopilot and reached for the basket. "Any sandwiches in there?"

"It's been a long day. Could we just forget what I said?" Kathy hoped he'd let it drop. "This will all be over soon anyway."

"No, we can't forget it." Trevor peeled back the covering on the sandwich she gave him. "I want an explanation."

When she didn't reply, he added, "Any time tonight will be just fine. I can wait!"

A dark mass off to their left whipped out of sight as the last of the clouds dropped away. All around them hung the deep velvet sky, quilted with millions of diamonds.

"Please, Trevor. I . . . I made a mistake. Don't make this more difficult for me," Kathy pleaded.

"If you had made a mistake, I'd be as understanding as possible."

"You mean I . . . I didn't make a mistake?"

"If you're talking about this," he said, running his right hand lightly up her arm and touching the nape of her neck, "no, you didn't make a mistake."

Kathy trembled in spite of her effort at control and tried to pull away, but there just wasn't any place to go. Warm color flooded her face as she fought the desire to let him continue. But reason won and she had to resist.

"Please, Trevor . . ."

"Please, Trevor, what?" he mocked her tone. "Please, Trevor, continue?" He openly laughed at her. "All right, I will." He pulled her toward him with strong fingers.

"Don't!" She pushed away. "Remember where we are!"

"You mean if we were on the ground I wouldn't have to stop? Okay, I'll land somewhere!" He reached for the autopilot switch, but Kathy covered it quickly with her hand.

"Don't you dare!" Fury was swiftly overtaking her embarrassment at his correct reading of her emotions. "I should never have let you take control of this airplane!"

"Mmm, maybe you're right," he countered, scanning the panel. A smile twitched at the corners of his mouth. "If you were flying, then I'd have all my attention on you," he teased.

"Ohhh," Kathy gritted her teeth. "If you treat all your women passengers like this, I feel sorry for Cynthia. Being married to you would be awful!"

Trevor made a couple of adjustments as they overflew Lewiston. The light of the beacon alternated green, white . . . green, white.

"What makes you so sure Cynthia is my wife?" He raised an eyebrow, but put both hands back on the controls.

Kathy straightened, visibly relieved that he had released her. "Isn't she?"

"Answer *my* question first!"

The moon sent a stray beam that silvered the wings and propeller. "It doesn't matter *why* I think it. Either she is your wife or she isn't."

"All right," Trevor sighed as though tired of bantering words. "If it makes any difference to you, she *isn't* my wife."

Kathy sucked in a sharp breath at his admission. "What is she then? Your fiancee? Girlfriend?"

"You tend to jump to a lot of conclusions! I think I can clear this up easily enough." Trevor started the descent into Joseph. "Cynthia, as you know, is a policewoman. But"— he adjusted the throttle again—"she's also my sister! That's why I was helping with this case. And a time or two she nearly gave away all my secrets—just to torture me in front of you!"

Kathy drained her cup to cover the emotional whirl his words spawned. The descent was smooth and direct as they sliced gracefully toward the lake and home.

Trevor crossed the airfield, announcing his intentions into the microphone. "Now, hang on to that cup so it doesn't break."

Touching down lightly, Trevor taxied to the parking area. A few dim figures could be seen outside the office. "Can you tie down the plane while I talk to the sheriff?"

"Sure," Kathy agreed. The way she felt, she could tie down the moon that was just tipping over the mountains. *Since he isn't in love with Cynthia,* Kathy mused as she deftly wielded the ropes, *then maybe he's—well, at least I know from the way he acted, he's attracted to me. I just wish he'd come right out and say what he's thinking.*

She carried their basket over to his waiting car and placed it behind the seat. On top she situated the special cup. "He's going to tell me what this means tonight," she muttered firmly, "or else!"

She'd started back toward the knot of people when Trevor broke away. "Over here, Kathy," he called. "The sheriff wants your signature. I told him you'd go in to the office tomorrow to make a statement."

"Where's Jed?" Kathy unconsciously stepped closer to Trevor and didn't question the comfort of his arm around her.

"He's already been taken into custody. You don't have to see him tonight."

The sheriff was courteous and to the point, and in a few minutes they were in the car and on their way back to the cabin. They drove silently around the curve and up to the lake, each lost in their own thoughts.

Suddenly Trevor braked and pulled into the beach area. Turning off the motor, he nervously tapped the steering wheel with his fingertips.

"Thanks for stopping. I do love this view of the lake." Kathy broke the silence after they'd sat for a few minutes. When he didn't respond, she tried another tack. "I suppose I'll be on my way home tomorrow if you're through with me."

"Come on." Trevor opened the door and climbed out. "Let's walk awhile." As they reached the edge of the water he put his arm around her and drew her firmly against his side. Slowing his steps to match hers, he ambled along the moist beach.

"Trevor, why did you need me?" Kathy voiced her puzzled thoughts. "I mean, if *you* could fly, why me?" She tilted her head up toward his face. The moonlight touched his cheeks and highlighted the strength of his chin.

"Let's not talk about business right now." He reached for her hand and intertwined their fingers.

At his tone and words, the moon took on a warm glow and touched her hair, spinning honey webs in the light breeze. At their feet the water lapped softly, kissed by moondrops.

Suddenly he stopped and stared into her eyes. The gentle grin had slipped into a strange look Kathy had never seen before. Her breath caught somewhere near her belt and the waves stood still.

Slowly, gently, he bent his head and brushed her lips with his. Softly they pressed together and the moon burst into a billion sparkles. Eons later he lifted his head a fraction of an inch. "I don't know what I was waiting for," he murmured, his mouth brushing her lips as he formed each word.

"I thought you'd never—"

His kiss stopped her words. This time his gentleness drew her deep into his embrace. Kathy slid her hands up around his neck, and his arms folded her securely.

Time swirled in a moon-silvered haze while the Wallowa Mountains pretended to sleep, allowing the two a private moment of bliss.

At last they reluctantly pulled apart. Trevor cradled her head beneath his chin and toyed with her golden hair.

"As much as I hate to say it," his voice held a strangely ragged edge, "I think we'd better go back. It must be very late."

Kathy raised a delicate wrist in an attempt to see her watch. But she was unable to read it, more from her whirling emotions than from blurred vision. "As far as I can tell," she turned so they could walk together on the beach, "it's beyond very late and is now *very early*."

"We have so much to talk about," Trevor's voice was husky, "but I guess it'll have to wait until tomorrow."

"It's already tomorrow," Kathy murmured dreamily, not wanting the moment to end.

"Even so, you'll still have to wait." He closed the car door when she was settled in the seat. Then, sliding in beside her, he snapped on the headlights, illuminating the gentle curve of the shore.

Kathy nestled her head comfortably on Trevor's shoulder as he turned the key to bring the engine to life. A moist kiss on the tip of her nose caught her by surprise.

She drew her breath in sharply, then let it out slowly as his warm lips trailed down to engulf her mouth. "I didn't know it could be like this," she murmured against his cheek when he reluctantly ended their kiss.

"We both have a lot to learn," Trevor replied, then shifted the car into gear. "But this isn't the time or the place."

———

In spite of her intentions, Kathy slept late the next morning. So much had happened in the past twenty-four hours that she could hardly take it all in. There were so many questions whirling through her head. But overriding all of them was the big question: what would her relationship with Trevor be today?

She fixed a light breakfast and tried to sort out her emotions, but concentrating was difficult. When noon came and passed with no sign of Trevor, Kathy finally decided to take matters into her own hands. Marching out to his camper, she pounded on his door.

"You've slept long enough," she called, banging loudly. "Come on, sleepyhead, get up!" She waited for his response, remembering the way he'd kissed the tip of her nose just as they'd said good-night. When he didn't answer, she knocked again and tried the doorknob. It opened easily.

"Trevor?" she called tentatively. "It's me, Kathy. Are you awake?"

An empty coffee cup sat in the sink and the twisted sheets revealed a vacant bed. Peering out the window, she noticed fresh tracks in the dust where his car had been parked.

"He must have gone to town." Kathy went outside and closed the door. Gazing at the mountains around her, she strolled down the rock-strewn dusty road. Overhead a blue jay bombed from tree to tree, raucously protesting her presence.

Automatically her feet turned in at the church campground. The area was quiet with no young children running about. Seeking an explanation and wondering where Professor Strauss was, she checked the main hall. A sign tacked by the door announced: College Retreat. That explained why there were no small children visible. Obviously they'd gone home, and the college-age group had taken over. Cautiously she opened the door and slipped into a seat near the back.

Professor Strauss was standing in front of the group of college-age campers. "We may not know what God's goal in our life is to be," he was saying. "But, we can honestly know we are called to follow Christ."

Kathy quickly tuned in to what he was saying.

"When we accept the truth that God knows what path we should take"—he pointed emphatically toward his Bible—"then we are no longer caught up in wondering where God is leading or why certain things happen. Rather, we can simply follow Him on a day-to-day basis."

He closed his Bible and picked it up. "The more you focus on Christ, the less you will focus on questions. Keep Him in clear view, and your questions will fade."

There were scuffling sounds as people pushed aside their chairs and went outside. Kathy waited until the professor was free from the cluster of people who stayed to talk after his session.

When he approached her, his face broke into a happy grin. "Kathy, how are things going for you?"

"Until yesterday I'd have said terrible." She greeted him with a smile as she fell into step beside him.

"And now?" He gave her a quizzical look.

"Incredible!"

"That's a quantum leap. What happened?"

"A couple of things," Kathy sighed, remembering. "The bad part is that my friend Jed was involved in stolen goods . . . and yesterday the police finally caught up with him." They went outside into the bright sun, and Kathy squinted in the sudden glare. "It turned out, Trevor—Mr. Kingston—was here on the investigation. He was on to Jed's activities all along."

"So the gruff Mr. Kingston was really a good guy after all."

"You might say that." Kathy couldn't help the blush that revealed her feelings. Trevor's kiss was still so fresh she tingled.

"Apparently there's more to this story than you've told me."

"Maybe . . . well, probably." She amended as he gave her a stern look. "I don't have the answers yet, but lots of questions."

"Seems I've heard you say that before," he laughed.

They reached the gate, and Kathy stepped outside. "I'll probably be going home today. At least I think I will. So I won't be stopping in anymore. But I wanted to tell you that I'm okay." She searched for words to express her thoughts. "I'm not struggling with the future anymore. I'm content to let God lead me one day at a time."

A huge smile spread across his face. "You're not going around in circles," he referred to the first day they'd met.

"You're right," she nodded, "I've learned it's much better to trust God and let Him lead me." She stepped away from him, waved, and turned back toward her cabin.

"I'll be praying for you," he called as she disappeared down the road.

Around the first bend in the road Kathy heard a crackling in the underbrush. She stopped to stare, and in a moment or two she was able to pick out a tiny fawn. Hidden by its mother, the baby was waiting for her next signal. Kathy turned away softly so that she wouldn't frighten the infant deer.

"Lord, I'm kind of like that," she prayed quietly as she sauntered back to her cabin, "just waiting for your next signal." A gentle peace seemed to lift some of the burden of her questions as she focused on Christ.

"About Trevor, Lord. You know how I feel about him, but I need your guidance to know what my next step should be. He seems so perfect, yet I don't know where he stands spiritually. We've never really had a chance to talk about it."

Remembering her miscalculations about Jed, she added, "I can't go any further in this relationship until I'm sure that Trevor loves you as much as I do."

Sidestepping the larger rocks, Kathy climbed the path to her cabin and was rewarded with a glimpse of Trevor's car parked beneath the trees.

17

"*I*t's about time you showed up," Trevor called from the porch where he stood watching her climb the hill.

Kathy grinned and waved at him. The sight of him urged her into a trot. She wanted to throw herself in his arms, feel his strength tighten around her, and most of all, drown in his kiss.

"I could say the same for you," Kathy panted, hurrying to meet him. "Where were you this morning?"

"Taking care of some business." He reached out to help her onto the porch. "If you'll pack, I'll drive you to town. The sheriff needs your statement before you leave."

"I'll be ready in a few minutes." Kathy was puzzled at Trevor's bruskness. She'd wondered what he would be like today, but somehow she hadn't anticipated this. From the gentle, loving, almost passionate Trevor of last night, he had suddenly changed into Mr. Kingston, the businessman.

While she was packing, Kathy carefully mulled over every detail of the last few days. But try as she might, she could find nothing that would cause Trevor to change so drastically.

"Aren't you ready yet?"

Kathy turned as Trevor stepped through her open bedroom door. "Yes, I think I've got everything." She handed him her suitcase, then ran to keep up with him as he strode quickly down the hall.

"I suppose you planned on leaving this behind?" Trevor

scooped up the horse and butterfly cup from the kitchen counter.

"No, I just haven't had time to check this room for my things."

"Come on, let's go." Trevor ushered her out and locked the door behind them. Silently she climbed into his car, and he stuffed her suitcase into the back along with the cup and his own luggage.

"Trevor," she confronted him cautiously as they drove along the lake, "is there anything wrong?"

"Wrong? No, of course not." He kept his eyes on the road.

"You seem . . . different." Kathy started to touch his arm and then decided against it. "I mean . . . last night—"

"Last night is past." He shook his head. "Today starts a whole new ball game."

Kathy stared hard out the window, turning her head so Trevor couldn't see how much she was fighting the tears. *So it was just the moonlight that made him kiss me*, she thought. *He never said he loved me. In fact, he never talked at all—just wanted to put off all my questions until today.*

Blinking rapidly to stop the tears from overflowing, Kathy's mind raced on. *Well, his attitude clearly shows how he feels. I was just a break at the end of a long and trying day.*

At the sheriff's office she quickly gave her statement and signed it.

"We'll be in touch with you, Miss Evans," the sheriff told her. "Thanks for all your help."

"I'm sorry it had to happen," Kathy shook her head. "But at least it's all over and I can go home. You have my address. Feel free to contact me anytime."

Outside, Trevor said nothing to her when she got into the car. He drove directly to the airport and parked by the log stumps that served as a fence.

Not wanting to prolong the agony, Kathy quickly

jumped out of the car and reached for her suitcase.

"Let me get that," Trevor said, trying to take it from her.

"That's all right, *Mr. Kingston*," Kathy emphasized his name, "I can carry my own things."

"Kathy, I . . ."

"I wouldn't want to trouble you." Kathy fished in her pocket for the airplane keys. "I've been enough trouble as it is." She slung the shoulder strap of her suitcase into place and hurried toward her airplane.

"Kathy, wait!" Trevor's footsteps sounded on the pavement behind her.

Kathy ignored him as long as she could. But flying wasn't like jumping into a car and driving off in a poof of dust, it took time to get ready.

"I said to *wait*." Trevor grabbed her shoulders and whirled her around. He dropped his hands as though touching her had burned him. "Explain this *Mr. Kingston* business," he demanded.

"You said today starts a whole new ball game. It's back to business." Kathy worked to keep her voice under control. "It's been nice flying for you, although I really think you could have handled the whole thing without me."

She unlocked the airplane and stowed her baggage in place. "If you ever need our services again, you know where to contact us."

Trevor stood there silently watching her perform her preflight duties. When she was finished and had climbed into the airplane, he walked up to the window, ducking under the wing.

"You forgot this." He held up the cup.

"You keep it," Kathy shook her head. "I don't know what your silly mystery is, and right now I really don't care." It wasn't true of course. She hadn't meant to leave the cup, but she needed to retain a little dignity right now.

"My mystery isn't silly," Trevor said slowly in a very

calm voice. "And I want you to take it. It's yours." He brushed her shoulders lightly as he reached through the window to place the cup on the seat opposite her. "Don't lose it," he admonished. "That cup is going to be important to you for the rest of your life."

"Arrogance becomes you," she retorted, angry that in spite of all that was happening his casual touch still sent tingles down her spine. "Now if you'll excuse me, I'm going to dig a hole in the sky."

"Sure thing," he patted her arm and backed away from the airplane. "Just remember it's blue up and green down!"

"Clear prop!" Kathy yelled and closed the window. His little joke about keeping the airplane right side-up made her feel like a seven-year-old.

The engine roared to life beneath her fingers, and Kathy was anxious to get airborne as quickly as possible. Lifting off at last, she turned left toward home, glancing back over her shoulder as the airport dropped behind her. She couldn't be sure, but just for a moment it looked like someone—maybe Trevor—was waving.

The afternoon heat provided a strong lift, and she was soon at altitude and leveled off. She hugged the ridge of mountains to her left in order to stay clear of the traffic pattern for other small airports in the valley. She scanned her instruments, then swept the sky from left to right, always on the alert for unreported traffic.

Glancing back inside the cabin again, her eyes caught the horse and butterfly cup. "If you could only talk," she wondered out loud. "What is your mystery?"

On course at last for home, Kathy deliberately pushed all thoughts of Trevor out of her mind and concentrated on flying. She noted the canyon opening that led to the Minam Horse Ranch and remembered that her mother wanted her to meet the new owner. But with all the trouble she'd had with Jed and Trevor this summer, Kathy wasn't in the mood to meet another man, no matter how fantastic Peggy said he was.

She crossed the mountains and dropped quickly into the valley beyond, noting the dusty summer haze. Harvest was in full swing, and the wheat fields were alive with combines and grain trucks. "I've missed so much." Kathy's eyes took in the scenery. While she'd been away the grain had passed from green to gold until its swelling heads bent heavy on the stalks. Just for the fun of it, she made three lazy circles, enjoying all the harvesting sights.

With each circle the magnetic pull of home and family grew, drawing her determinedly to the Pendleton airport.

"Home at last!" She touched down lightly and taxied in, anxious to see the look of welcome on her father's face.

But only the fuel boy was there to welcome her. He said her father was out on another charter and wouldn't be home until tomorrow. Kathy tied down the plane and bypassed the office, suddenly wanting nothing more than the comfort of being home. It wasn't until she put her suitcase and the cup into her car that Kathy remembered Peggy's stuffed bear.

"Oh no! I must have left it in the closet." She flopped down into the driver's seat. "If Trevor hadn't pushed me so fast, I wouldn't have forgotten it."

No matter how hard she tried to forget it, the missing bear seemed to dampen her homecoming. Asking Trevor to bring it to her was just as much out of the question as flying back to get it. Peggy would just have to wait for her gift or do without it completely!

"Lord," she prayed, leaning against the steering wheel, "it seems as if things aren't going very well today. First the change in Trevor and my disappointment in not seeing Dad, and now forgetting my gift for Peggy. I know they're just little things, but help me to let go of them and focus on you. Amen."

As she drove down the winding road to the bottom of the hill, Kathy found her thoughts running ahead to the next days and weeks in her life. *I'm almost back where I was before I went to Wallowa Lake—no purpose, no calling.*

She turned onto the freeway that led toward home. *But at least I've learned a thing or two.* She glanced at her reflection in the rearview mirror. *I know more than ever that I need God in my life, and that I need to be careful who I fall in love with.*

A deep peace seemed to settle on her heart as she turned into the family driveway. There would be many opportunities to serve God right here—all she had to do was watch for them. "Maybe Lacey will help me think of ideas," she thought out loud.

Then a sudden thought startled her. *Maybe Lacey is the reason for the change in Trevor.* Her mind whirled. *He really seemed to like her, and he seemed like the kind of guy who would react to whichever woman was handy. Maybe I was just handy last night. Maybe it's really Lacey he wants.*

She slowed the car, wondering if she was jumping to conclusions again or if it could be true. She wondered how she'd handle it if it was. Turning into the driveway, she allowed the car to roll to a stop.

"Kathy!" Peggy bounded out of the door and ran toward her sister, long chestnut hair streaming behind her. "You're home!"

"Obviously!" Kathy jumped out of the car and into her sister's arms. "This time I'll hang around for a while, if that's okay with you."

"It's about time." Peggy gave her sister a hug. "Can I get your suitcase?"

"Uh-huh," Kathy nodded. "It's on the backseat. Where's Mom?"

"In the kitchen. Where else?"

Kathy turned toward the back door, lifting her damp

hair off the back of her neck. August in Pendleton was hot and the temperature change from the lake was very noticeable.

"Hey, what's this?" Peggy caught up to Kathy as she entered the house. In one hand she held the horse and butterfly cup, twisting it to examine it thoroughly.

"Oh that," Kathy carefully schooled her voice into a casual tone. "It's just a souvenir from the lake. A gift from my employer." If she let even one thought of Trevor stray into her mind, she knew she'd betray her true feelings.

"What was he like?" Peggy plunked the suitcase against the kitchen wall and straddled a chair, still holding the cup.

"Who?" Their mother caught the last question, then enveloped her older daughter in a welcoming hug.

"The guy Kathy worked for," Peggy explained while her mother brushed a strand of hair out of Kathy's eyes. "Well, Kathy, what was he like?"

"By your standards," Kathy kept her tone noncommittal, "old and a bit stuffy."

"Yuck! Sounds awful!" Peggy shoved the cup across the table toward Kathy. "I'll bet you're glad to be home and away from him."

"You're right. I *am* glad to be home," Kathy agreed, trying to ignore how lost she felt knowing she'd never see Trevor again—or wondering if she'd see him as Lacey's husband.

"Why don't you get settled." Her mother gave her a questioning look that said she could see something was hurting her daughter. "Dinner will be ready in about an hour. You can tell us all about your job then."

Kathy picked up her suitcase and the cup and gratefully escaped Peggy's pointed questions as she closed the door to her room. Unpacking was easy, but filled with too many memories.

Why did her empty suitcase smell like the damp leaves

on that early morning walk on the mountain with Trevor? Her sweater bore a slight smoke tang from the evening campfires they'd often shared. And that cup! It brought back so many memories.

Angry at herself for allowing the past to cloud her homecoming, Kathy glared at herself in the mirror. An uncontrolled tear traced its way down her cheek. As the salty moisture touched her lips, memory avalanched her to the beach and the taste of Trevor's kiss.

There was to be no escape. It would be a long evening, a long summer—a long lifetime—without Trevor.

———

The next morning Kathy was pleasantly surprised to see her father at the breakfast table. "I thought you weren't due home until later today," she greeted him with a hug.

"Is that any kind of a welcome for your father?" he teased, returning her hug. "If you like, I could leave and come back later," he mocked a hurt look.

"Don't be silly, Dad." Kathy poured herself a cup of coffee and accepted the plate of toast from her mother. "I'm just glad you're here."

When they'd finished eating, Kathy poured them each another cup of coffee and perched on the edge of her chair. "Dad, we need to talk about my job status."

"Are you quitting?"

"No, of course not. I'd like to stay if our finances can support me."

"If you were to leave, I'd have to hire a part-time pilot and someone to help in the office. So, if you want it, the job is still yours."

"Thanks, Dad. It's exactly what I want." Kathy patted his arm and began to relax. "I just hope there aren't too many more jobs like this last one."

"A bit tough on you, was it?" He leaned back in his chair, watching her closely.

"Not my favorite thing to do." Kathy stirred her cup absently, staring into the brown swirl without seeing it.

"Want to talk about it?" His voice was low and soothing.

"Maybe later." Kathy pushed back from the table and carried her dishes to the sink. "Right now I think both of us are late for work."

"Late or not, I always have time for my daughter." He stood up and put his cap on his head. "But if you want to wait, I'll be ready to listen whenever you're ready to talk."

They drove in separate cars to the airport, and Kathy quickly plunged into her job. The paper work had piled up tremendously in her absence. Obviously her dad had done only the minimum, leaving the bulk of the office work for her.

Over the next few days Kathy dropped into a routine of leaving early for work and using the quiet time before business began to read her Bible and pray. Every day this quiet time became more and more important to her. The Bible seemed fresh and new, almost as if she'd never really read it before.

By Saturday things were under control, and Kathy had a few minutes to just relax. Guilt touched her as she thought how she'd ignored Lacey, or at least put off letting her know she was back in town. She'd excused herself a dozen times with as many reasons, but the truth was she was afraid she would learn that Lacey and Trevor were dating.

Kathy stared at the phone, trying to force herself to call Lacey, but her fears won and she yielded to cowardice. After lunch she had a clear desk and decided to check on the mail.

"Be back in a minute," she called to her father as she went out the door. It was a hot muggy day that promised a storm. The humidity was high and the air was absolutely still. Kathy glanced toward the sky and saw a storm cell moving in from the south.

Retrieving the mail from the box, she sorted through it as she strolled back to the office. Suddenly she stopped dead, her heart pounding. An envelope with Trevor's firm handwriting stood out from all the rest. But disappointment nearly made her cry as she noticed it was addressed to her father—not her.

Forcing the tears back, she swallowed hard. *He could have written to me by now . . . or called.* She blinked fast to clear the blurring in her eyes. *But he hasn't. I guess I hoped for too much.*

Deliberately forcing her steps back to the office, she continued sorting the mail. But it was with a heavy heart that she handed her father his stack of envelopes and took the rest to her desk.

"Most of these were just routine." Her father handed her his opened mail a few minutes later. "And this one"—he handed her Trevor's letter—"has a check in it for your services. It says that your work was satisfactory, and that he would be pleased to recommend you as a pilot anytime."

"That's nice." Kathy turned away from him to her computer. "I'll take care of those letters in a few minutes." She swallowed hard, praying her father wouldn't see the pain she felt at Trevor's strictly business letter.

"Honey." He touched the back of her shoulder lovingly. "Don't you think it's time we had that talk?"

"There's not much to say, Dad. The job's over, and I—"

18

"*I* think there's plenty to say," he interrupted. "I've been patient long enough."

With that firm tone in his voice, Kathy knew it would be best to start talking. Slowly, painfully she told him all that had happened. Beginning with her uneasiness at Trevor's brusk attitude toward her and her confusion about the job, she included all the details of Jed's trouble with the law.

She left out the real problem, though. She didn't mention Lacey, or how vacant her life was now that Trevor was gone. There were some things she just couldn't share with her father. At least, not yet.

Ending with Jed's arrest, she finished, "It was just about the most difficult thing I've ever had to do, Dad. I . . . I wish it had been someone else."

"I know that. And perhaps I was wrong to send you." He shook his graying head. "But I still think you were the best person for the job."

"You knew what this job was all about?" Kathy looked up in surprise.

"I'm afraid so, honey." He tapped his fingers on her desk top. "But Trevor insisted that you be told nothing. You see, Jed had used me a couple of times to transport packages. You know we always help if we can." He looked out the window at the approaching storm cell with unseeing eyes. Although it was closer, it appeared to be moving slowly around them toward the mountains.

"I met the guy you called Frank and began to get suspicious, but Jed's always been such a likeable sort that I had a difficult time believing he was involved in anything even slightly shady."

"Especially when you knew how I felt about him?" Kathy got up and walked to the window.

"That was probably the main reason I knew I had to do something about it." Her father stared hard at his fingertips. "If he was innocent, I wanted him to be fully in the clear. But if he was involved, I didn't want him to hurt you somewhere down the line."

Father and daughter were both silent for a few minutes, each lost in thought, searching their own memories.

"Dad," Kathy broke softly into their reflections. "You called Mr. Kingston Trevor. Why? Have you known him long?"

"I . . . that is, we got together several times as we discussed just how to handle this situation." Her dad got up to join her at the window. "It took a lot of planning, a lot of thought, and a lot of prayer."

"So that's why you didn't hesitate to have me stay so long with him." Kathy cocked her head in his direction. "You knew him pretty well, didn't you?"

"You know I'd never send you into that kind of situation if I hadn't trusted the man completely."

"I knew I could trust your judgment, but for a while there it was tough." Kathy was glad she hadn't told anyone, not even her father, about her feelings for Trevor.

"Maybe this is sticking my nose where it shouldn't be"—he reached out and lifted her chin with his big calloused hands—"but how are you handling the emotions? You and Jed were pretty close."

"You told me to be very sure before I made any kind of decision about him." Kathy smiled into his concerned eyes. "I asked God to show me the truth, and although it hurt, I found out for sure that I don't love him . . . probably never did."

"Thank you, Lord," her father murmured. "Your mother and I have been praying for you, Kathy."

She reached out with her tiny hands and curled them around his strong ones. "It's really great having a dad like you. Thanks for caring." She raised up on her tiptoes and kissed his weathered cheek.

"And what about Trevor?" he added softly. "How do you feel about him?"

"What's there to say?" Kathy backed away from him, lowering her eyes. "He hired me for his business and," she raised a shoulder in a gentle shrug, "he was a businessman when I left him." She walked back to her desk and hoped she'd held her voice steady enough that her dad wouldn't probe further.

"Just checking." He started down the hall toward his office and stopped partway. "It's pretty quiet this afternoon. Why don't you take the rest of the day off? Go on home and tell your mother to have an early dinner. I'll get there as soon as I can."

"I'll take that anytime, boss." Kathy laughed in relief.

"By the way, honey," he added, "congratulations. That was a job well done—worthy of any son if I do say so myself!"

"One of these days," she playfully retorted, "you're going to figure out that I'm your daughter, not your *son*. I wonder if you'll be able to handle the shock!"

She chuckled at his answering shrug and gathered up her purse. Outside again, Kathy noted that although the storm had moved past them, the air was still hot. With thoughts of a dip in their neighbor's swimming pool, she hurried home.

"Peggy," she called as she passed her sister's room, where the younger girl was sprawled on the bed, reading a novel. "Want to go swimming?"

"Soon as I finish this chapter," Peggy answered without looking up. "I'm just at the good part."

"According to you, all the parts are good." Kathy chuckled and went in search of her swimming suit. This would be a good time to start building a deeper relationship with her sister.

Both girls were soon stretched out comfortably on floating chairs in their neighbor's pool. Although no one was at home, they had a standing invitation to use the pool.

"Kathy." Peggy was vigorously rubbing sunscreen on her delicate skin. "Mom said Jed got into some kind of trouble and won't be coming over here anymore. Is that really true?"

"Of course it's true or Mom wouldn't have said it." Kathy, too, was smoothing tanning lotion on her already golden legs and arms.

"But aren't you in love with him?"

"I almost made a terrible mistake, Peggy." Kathy leaned back in the chair and pulled sunglasses over her eyes. "I nearly confused friendship for love. And, believe me, the two aren't the same thing at all!"

"How can you tell the difference?"

"That's a tough one to answer." It seemed Peggy had been asking why, how, or what since she'd been two years old. "Until you experience the real thing, love is kind of hard to define. I had to do a lot of praying to be absolutely sure." They drifted in the sun, letting the water rock and swirl them around the pool.

"If you aren't in love with Jed, then who *are* you in love with?" Peggy dragged her hands in the water.

Kathy's eyes flew open. Trying to make her voice sound casual, she asked, "What makes you think I'm in love with someone?" Mentally she chastised herself for making that slip of the tongue.

"I may be only sixteen, but I'm not stupid." Peggy flicked a few drops of water at Kathy. They sizzled on her hot skin and evaporated in the sun. "You *are* in love, aren't you?"

"Even if I am, and I'm not saying that I am"—Kathy closed her eyes to concentrate on her words—"there's nothing happening, so don't get all excited."

"Was it someone you met up at the lake?"

"I met someone interesting, yes."

"What's he like?"

"Persistent little thing, aren't you?" Kathy flicked some water back at her sister. "Okay, so I met someone special," she crumbled the thin barrier she'd tried to erect.

"Did he kiss you?"

"You're getting too personal," Kathy warned, but memories of Trevor's kiss sent flames racing across her cheeks.

"He did, I know he did!" Peggy warmed up to her subject. "It was in the moonlight, down at the lake. I know it was. It just had to be. And he's madly in love with you—and he's going to whisk you away to his castle in Scotland! Can I come and visit you? Can I be in the wedding?"

"Hold it, Peggy. You've been reading too many novels. It wasn't quite like that." Kathy splashed her sister again.

"It was more like this ordinary guy—you know the kind, business suit, hard-working—asked me to do some typing for him. And maybe the part by the lake is true, but there isn't any castle in Scotland—and there won't be any wedding."

She sighed heavily. "You see, just because I fell in love with him doesn't mean he feels the same way about me. Sorry to prick your pink balloon, but that's the way it is."

"I'm sorry too," Peggy sounded older for just a moment. "It must hurt something awful to love someone and not be loved back."

Kathy didn't answer; the pain was too fresh, too real.

"Maybe this is the wrong time to say anything, but Mom's still hoping you'll want to meet the guy from the Minam Horse Ranch." Peggy slipped off her chair into the water. "I've met him, and he's really nice."

"I'm not really in the mood to meet him, thanks." Kathy pictured the kind of person who would buy a ranch out in the middle of nowhere. Dull, plodding, probably even a bit of a recluse. Somehow he just couldn't measure up to Trevor.

"He always goes to church with us whenever he's here," Peggy went on as though she hadn't heard Kathy's answer. "And he's a real neat Christian. Pastor even had him preach one Sunday, but it wasn't like a real sermon, just talking."

She swam to the edge of the pool. "All the kids really like him, and you can understand what he says about God and the Bible. If Dad'll let me, I want to go up there some- time and stay at his ranch for a camp."

"I'll tell you what." Kathy slid into the water up to her neck, enjoying the cool, refreshing sensation. "You go on up to his ranch—I'll even fly you there. Maybe he'll fall in love with you and get you out of my hair!" She playfully splashed her sister with both hands to start a water fight.

"He's too old for me, or I would." Peggy sputtered and turned to dunk Kathy with both hands. "Besides, I met my someone special last year at the beach."

"Oh yes. I remember—your mystery man." Kathy went under the water as Peggy pushed hard. She came up gig- gling and sputtering. "The entire time we were at the ocean, you talked about him constantly, but you never let me meet him. In fact, I don't think he ever existed except in your fantasy world."

"But he *is* real. You'll see. Someday I'll marry him, then you'll have to eat those words!"

Both girls were enjoying the fray. They dove and splashed, teased and chased, until they dropped with exhaustion. Kathy felt more relaxed than she had all summer. It was good to be home, good to have a sister like Peggy. Already she could tell her relationship with her sister had improved.

Finally the girls dragged themselves out of the water, making wet body marks on the hot cement surrounding the pool. Chlorine fumes filled their nostrils as they stretched out to dry in the sun. It would soon be time to help their mother with dinner. But for now, it was great to just relax.

"Really, Kathy." Peggy helped her put away the floating chairs when they'd stayed in the sun long enough. "If you love him—whoever he is—*that* much, why are you just sitting here? I mean, I'd go track him down—*make* him love me."

"It sounds as if it would be easy," Kathy responded, "but I hoped he'd see just how much he missed me and come after me."

"That only happens in books."

Peggy's insight was almost shocking. "I know. But to be honest, I don't know for sure where he stands spiritually. That's the most important. I just couldn't marry someone who wasn't doing what God wants him to."

"You're so strong, Kathy." Peggy's voice was wistful. "I don't think I'm that strong. I think love would win out, and I'd marry him anyway. Maybe he'd become a Christian after we got married."

"Oh, baby sister"—Kathy hugged her before they went in the house—"a man's relationship with God is the most important part of him." Kathy was amazed the words flowed so easily out of her mouth. "If you ask God's help, He'll give you the strength to wait for the right man."

They dropped off their wet things in the laundry room, and Kathy started a load of clothes washing while Peggy used the shower. When it was her turn, Kathy let the tepid water wash away all the chlorine and thoroughly shampooed her hair. Then, wrapping her head turban-fashion with a big fluffy bath towel, she tied her green silk robe firmly around her. She wandered toward the living room to pick up the newspaper before she dried her hair.

A knock on the front door made Kathy whirl around for her mother, but she was nowhere in sight. The hum of a hair dryer told her Peggy wouldn't hear if she called. There was nothing to do but answer the door herself.

"It's probably just one of Peggy's friends anyway," she reasoned, tying the belt to her robe tighter and reaching for the doorknob.

"Lovely! Do you always dress like that?"

Kathy stood stock-still at the sight of Trevor standing on her front porch. As the shock wore off, she realized how ridiculous he looked holding Peggy's oversized bear under one arm.

"Come in," she finally invited, stepping aside to let him in. "I'd hate to have our neighbors see how weird our friends are. And speaking of looks," she added, "do you always run around with a bear under your arm?" She stifled a giggle, noticing for the first time how tired he looked. She scanned him carefully, drinking in every detail from a smudge of grass stain on his jeans to the casual open neck of his soft yellow shirt.

"At least you called me a friend." Trevor stepped into the room and perched on the arm of her father's recliner. "The last time I talked to you, I wasn't so sure."

"I . . . that is, things weren't—"

"It doesn't matter," Trevor interrupted. "Let's just start fresh today."

"Thanks for bringing the bear. I didn't miss it until I was all the way home." Suddenly conscious of how she was dressed, Kathy took the stuffed animal from him. Brushing passed him, she curled up on the couch, tucking her robe around her and clutching the bear on her lap.

Trevor turned, following her with his eyes. "You look fine. Are you?"

"Just great," she stretched the truth only a little bit. "And you?"

"To tell you the truth, lousy!" He stood up and stuffed his hands in his pockets. "You can't believe the follow-up work on that case. And then there was all the work I've neglected this summer just to concentrate on that one project." He raised one hand, palm up. "Kathy, I honestly tried to get over here sooner, but I just couldn't."

Kathy didn't know if it was the look on his face, the pleading in his voice, or just because she couldn't keep from touching him any longer. Whatever it was, she found herself scrambling off the couch.

"Trevor, I know—"

"So do I!" He rushed to meet her.

The towel slipped off her head and dropped unheeded to the floor as he wrapped his arms around her. Drops from her wet hair ran in rivulets down his neck, but neither of them seemed to notice as their lips met in soft satisfaction.

"Oh, how I've missed you," he murmured against her cheek when he stopped kissing her long enough to breathe. "I just wish I could stay longer."

"But you just got here," Kathy protested as she started to rest her head on his shoulder. Realizing that she was getting him wet, she lifted her head quickly and looked up at him. "Can't you stay? I'd like you to meet my family."

A smile played at the corner of Trevor's mouth as his arms tightened around her again. "Not today. But I'll be in town tomorrow. I'll stop by in the afternoon."

19

Sunday morning dawned bright and beautiful as only an Oregon August morning can be. Kathy hummed as she prepared for church and was surprised when she realized she was singing the song the children had sung at camp.

"Let God do it. Trust and obey." She sang the simple words softly. "Let God do it. He knows the way." Over and over the little melody rang in her heart.

I am trying to trust and obey, Lord. I know your way is best for me. Kathy's eyes fell on the horse and butterfly cup and her heart skipped a beat. *God, would you please give a clear sign of where Trevor stands with you?* She picked up her Bible and hurried out to join her family.

"Thanks again for the bear," Peggy bubbled as they wound their way down the hill through the streets to their church. "I just love it!"

Everywhere there were bright banners stretched across the streets proclaiming the coming world-famous Pendleton Roundup. But Kathy hardly saw the colorful rodeo signs, she was concentrating so fully on seeing Trevor again today.

As they slipped quietly into a church pew Peggy leaned over and whispered to Kathy, "You get to meet him—Mom says he's coming to dinner today."

"Who?" Kathy raised her eyebrow.

"The guy from the Minam Horse Ranch—the one I've been telling you about."

Kathy shrugged her shoulders indifferently and sighed.

Why did he have to come today when her whole mind was occupied with thoughts of Trevor?

They were singing the first hymn when a rustle at her end of the row caught her attention. Kathy broke off mid-note in shock. Trevor, dressed in a deep blue suit and sparkling white shirt, was sidestepping his way to the empty seat beside her.

"Sorry I'm late," he whispered as though she ought to have expected him. Then grasping her hymnal with a firm hand, his rich baritone voice joined her soprano in singing. It took effort and control to calm the sudden pounding of her heart. For once she hardly knew whether she sang on key or even what the words were.

His arm rested comfortably behind her on the back of the bench as they listened to the announcements.

"We have two of our favorite guests with us today," the pastor's voice broke into her thoughts. "Professor Strauss is here on his way back to the college after having spent the summer at Wallowa Lake."

Kathy twisted her head to see where the professor was seated. But with all the other heads and necks craning in that direction she couldn't quite catch sight of him.

"And also with us is Trevor Kingston from the Minam Horse Ranch. Trevor, would you join me here on the platform and lead us in prayer as we begin our worship service?"

Kathy sat stunned as Trevor got to his feet and wended his way to the front of the church. It couldn't be! Kathy struggled to put all the pieces together.

Of course, Kathy thought, standing with the congregation for prayer, *that's why he gave me the horse cup. He wanted me to know about the horse ranch. But why didn't he tell me sooner?* Trevor's voice booming from the pulpit interrupted her thoughts as he earnestly sought God's guidance for the morning service. Hearing him pray sent a thrill through her heart.

As each of them followed the pastor's scripture references in their own Bible, Kathy noticed that Trevor's Bible was well worn and thoroughly marked with notes and underlines, much like her own recently underlined Bible. The condition of his Bible and the depth of his prayer seemed to confirm that here was a man in close communion with God.

"Thank you, Lord," she whispered during the benediction, "that Trevor knows you so well."

Outside after the service, they shook hands with their friends, then Trevor tugged her gently toward his car.

"Come on," he urged. "We've got some talking to do before we go home."

"Actually," Kathy grinned, sliding into the front seat, "most of my questions don't seem to be quite as important as I thought they were."

"But I have some things I need to say," Trevor countered. He started the engine and drove away slowly. At first he just wandered around the streets, and then, with a bit more purpose, he directed the car toward the airport.

"I talk better around airplanes," he explained. They parked in the public parking lot and Trevor led her through the wire gate that segregated the private airplanes from the commercial area.

"Speaking of airplanes . . ." Kathy snuggled her hand deeper into his. "You never answered my question about why you needed me to fly. You're such a good pilot. Why me?"

"Actually, it wasn't you I asked for." Trevor slowed his steps and they sauntered from one parked airplane to another. The planes sat in neat rows, waiting for someone to release them into the sky.

"We needed someone Jed would trust." Trevor ducked

under a Tri-Pacer's wing. "And since he didn't know me, I knew he wouldn't try to use me. Your dad said he'd send me somebody Jed knew."

They peered through the windows of an old Champ, enjoying the aging instrument panel. "In fact, I'd flown over to talk to your dad several times," Trevor continued. "When everything was set, he assured me that one of his pilots would do the work."

"That's why you were so shocked when I showed up?" Kathy took his hand as their path wove between a blue 182 and a brown 152.

"Right. I'd seen your picture, but I could have cheerfully choked your dad. He knew it was a dangerous operation, and to send a woman—his own daughter . . ." Trevor's arm tightened protectively around her. "That's why I didn't tell you what was happening right away. I tried to get your dad to change his mind."

"Dad was right." Kathy leaned her head against his shoulder as they paused in front of a Piper Cub. "I was the most logical person."

"He finally convinced me, but by then I knew I needed reinforcements. You, my love," he traced the outline of her nose, "weren't being exactly cooperative, if you'll remember."

They moved on to check out a Tomahawk, but Kathy couldn't concentrate on anything but Trevor's voice.

"That's when I called Cynthia and decided to bring her down to Joseph." Trevor turned Kathy into the curve of his arm. "Besides, I thought she might divert Jed's attention."

"She did a good job," Kathy agreed, remembering the scene outside her window at the lake. "I thought you both were drooling over her."

"She embarrassed me mostly; I've never seen her act so sexy. But right now, the only one I'm drooling over is you." He bent slightly and brushed her cheek with his lips.

"I think . . ." He lifted her chin with his fingers. "I think," he repeated, "we'd better go and see your father."

"Right now?" Still tingling from his touch, Kathy reluctantly turned to angle back toward the car.

"Right now!" Trevor nodded. "After all, he did this on purpose, and he may as well be the first to know."

"The first to know what?" Kathy gazed up into his face at the strange tone in his voice.

"That his plan worked." Trevor opened the door of the car and helped her in. "He knew we'd be going through a lot together."

"You're right!" Kathy exclaimed as the last piece of the puzzle fit together. "At least he had this part all planned." She tilted her head back and laughed.

"I thought you'd agree. He's quite a matchmaker." Trevor traced the tip of her nose with his finger. "Your sister showed me your picture a dozen times, and your mother was always talking about you—what you were doing, what you were *going* to do. I should have seen it coming!"

"Do you know, I didn't figure out the mystery of the horse cup until this morning." She kissed his fingertips and reluctantly allowed him to start the car. "I should have guessed sooner that it meant the horse ranch."

"I tried to tell you that the day we were on the mountain," he nodded. "By then it was too late to tell you exactly who I was—and I was so much in love with you, I had to do something."

"You were what?" Kathy gasped. She'd only hoped that his kisses meant as much to him as they did to her.

"That's right—in love with you. Totally swept off my feet by a beautiful, hazel-eyed, honey gold blond picture-come-to-life!" He drove out of the parking lot. "And if I stop to kiss you again to prove it, we'll never get to see your dad today."

He braked gently for the first curve. "In fact, the day you

left the lake I tried everything I could to keep from telling you how I felt. I knew if I touched you even once that morning I'd never be able to concentrate on finishing up all that business with Jed."

"The promise of the butterfly . . . if I'd only understood." Kathy scooted across the seat and laid her head on his shoulder. "The butterfly on the cup meant there was a new life coming if I'd just be patient."

"The butterfly is a symbol of the new life God promises us, a promise of His love . . . and mine." Trevor's fingers relaxed their grip on the steering wheel as though a great burden had been lifted from his shoulders.

"I wish you'd told me sooner." Kathy's eyes were bright with tears of joy.

"I wanted to," a soft sigh escaped his lips. "But just when I thought I could—in fact I'd just told Cynthia that I was going to tell you the whole truth—you tossed in that bit about being such close friends with Jed!"

"I didn't know she was your sister. That's why you were standing so close to her after we came down from the mountain." Kathy shook her head at all their misunderstandings. "I only said that to mask my own feelings. I was so sure you were in love with her."

A mental picture of the Joseph Days Parade invaded her thoughts. "But something has me puzzled," she frowned. "What about Lacey? You really seemed to hit it off with her."

"Actually, Lacey and I had met here at church last winter." He negotiated the last curve on the hill. "It was all we could do to keep from telling you that we already knew each other. She had told me so much about you."

"And I was green with envy. I decided you had fallen for her." Kathy shook her head. "That Lacey, when I see her again I'll . . . I'll give her a piece of my mind. The agony you and she put me through!"

Then, as she regained a sense of reality, she couldn't help but tease him a bit. "Were you jealous of Jed?" She batted her long lashes, secure in her new knowledge of his love.

"Outrageously!" He pulled over and parked at the bottom of the hill. "You're as impossible as your dad." Trevor bent to kiss her swiftly.

There was a new sparkle in his eyes as he raised his head. "Would your parents be really upset if we didn't show up for dinner?"

"Under the circumstances"—Kathy thought about all the plotting that had gone into getting them together—"I don't think there'd be a problem."

Trevor turned the car around and started back up the hill.

"Everybody knew who you were but me." Kathy shook her head in amazement. "By the way, where are we going?"

"Let's fly out to the ranch." This time Trevor parked by their office. "I want you to see it. After I found it last year, I couldn't get out of the insurance business fast enough to settle in that beautiful canyon."

Trevor followed her into the office while she telephoned home to say they wouldn't be coming for dinner. Then they hurried toward the flight line.

Kathy untied the knots she'd tied so carefully in an effort to chain her airplane to the earth. They both preflighted the plane in swift, sure movements. As Trevor ran a practiced hand swiftly along the propeller, Kathy reached out and touched its edge too, allowing her fingers to intertwine with his.

"If you distract me, we'll never get there." He tried to sound gruff without succeeding. "Now get into that airplane before I change my mind."

"Uh—just a minute." Kathy's eyes sparkled with mischief. "Who's flying, you or me?"

"I am! And don't you forget it," Trevor grinned, firmly shoving her toward the passenger side. "You'll have lots of time to fly after we get settled at the ranch."

"Moving kind of fast, aren't you?" Kathy closed her own door behind her and locked it. Now she knew exactly where she fit into God's plan. Professor Strauss had been right. She wasn't going in circles anymore.

"I didn't hear any objections." He paused before inserting the key, a frown touched his eyes. "There aren't any—I mean, you don't . . ."

"I love you, if that's what you want to know." Kathy leaned across the seat, brushing his shoulder with her lips and locking his door at the same time. "And don't you try to get away. It's much too late for that! Peggy wants to be a bridesmaid, and I have no intentions of disappointing her."

Trevor sighed contentedly and started the engine as Kathy reached out to rest her hand on his. Their plane taxied down the runway and lifted on butterfly wings into their new life filled with promise.